French Lessons

The Art of Living
and Loving Well!

Third edition September 2013
First edition July 2013

Published by Penciled In
296 Higuera Street
San Luis Obispo, CA 93401
penciledin.com

ISBN 13:   978-1939502063

Book Design by Ben Lawless

Cover Design by Jeff Love and Ben Lawless
Using photographs by Leslie Pujiono & Bob Smith

Text is set in MrsVonEckley,
Avenir Next and Adobe Caslon

French Lessons

The Art of Living and Loving Well!

E. J. Gore

Penciled In

For Manuel...
The Paris of my heart...

And for my darling Mother...
14 Sept 1922–8 Feb 2013

Contents

Gabrielle...

Gabrielle...

On an April afternoon in a café near the Jardin de Luxembourg, I'm celebrating my second day in Paris by ordering a *Kir Royale.*

A bemused waiter places the glass before me with a flourish and my spirits rise like the bubbles swirling upward through the champagne and cassis. The late day sun shifts through a nearby window just enough to light up the rose colored flute and I take this as a favorable omen. I may be at something of a crossroads in my life, but at least I've arrived there in Paris.

The champagne fizzes and tickles my nose in perfect accompaniment to my excitement. And I must confess I am the tiniest bit nervous as well. I have a rendezvous of sorts.

The afternoon before my departure from New York for Paris, in the midst of frantic last minute packing, I'd had a sudden visit from Mitzi, my erstwhile and adorable godmother. She'd rushed breathlessly through the door in her usual flurry of scarves, shopping bags and tinkling bracelets.

"Precious girl, I'm so late to Kenny, he'll refuse to ever do my hair again for the rest of my life," she pauses dramatically gesturing toward an already perfect coiffure, "but I simply had to give you this for Paris!" she waves an overly scented pale pink envelope toward me. I reach for it and she whips it away, "No, no. Wait! First,

I must tell you about Gabrielle!"

Gabrielle LaCroix, wife of a diplomat was the epitome of an elegant French woman, as well as one of considerable intelligence, charm and wit, who Mitzi had come to "know and adore" while living in Paris some years ago. To have her as a friend Mitzi explains, is "not only a great advantage socially, but such fun! My dear, she knows everyone, goes everywhere. Or she used to before Charles passed away. She prefers a quieter life now. We still keep in touch but I hear from her less."

After Mitzi and I get into a gentle argument about whether I'll call on her friend, she trumps me as she stands to leave with a "Darling! Who else do you know in Paris? Besides, with things as they are, well... you know how they are, it might not hurt to have a friend," a shrug of her shoulders.

So here I sit, having telephoned Gabrielle who's said she'd be delighted to meet for an early dinner this evening. I finish my drink then make my way to the *Brasserie Balzac* on the rue des Écoles.

I enter the *Balzac* and stand looking around at a pleasant room hung with colorful paintings. Crisp white linens cover each table as waiters in long aprons bustle to and fro. The background music is the buzz of left bank habitués arguing with each other over carafes of wine.

A maitre-d in a black tailcoat materializes beside me. "Madame Purcell?" and at my nod, leads me to a banquette in a distant, cozy corner. The attractive, impeccably groomed woman waiting there, a tiny dog upon her lap, looks up, her eyes alight. "Suzanne, it must be!" I nod and take the proffered hand, smooth as silk.

"And I am Gabrielle. This is Joie." The little dachshund looks up at me shyly, tail barely moving.

"Suzanne is one of my most favorite names," she confides as I'm seated.

"*Merci.*" It's now one of mine as well, I immediately prefer it to Susan.

I hand her Mitzi's letter which she places in her handbag.

"*Merci.* I shall look forward to reading it later."

Gabrielle orders wine, *Vouvray*, which is brought forward, tasted, poured. It's a light white wine, with a hint of fruit, perfect for a Spring evening. We toast Mitzi, then begin to chat, the sort of conversation women fall into so effortlessly, all over the world.

At some point Gabrielle glances downward to pat Joie and asks, "So what is it that brings you to Paris, Suzanne?"

"Well," I edit my answer, "I've loved Paris all my life. But I've only been here for a week or two before." I move my glass back and forth across the white cloth, "I've always wondered what it would be like to live here, at least for a few months. And now... now circumstances have conspired and I have the chance—to live here and write about it."

"You are a writer!"

"No. Well, yes, a writer of sorts. I've marketed pharmaceuticals for several years now. But while I'm here I'll get to be a bit more creative. I'm writing a series of articles on Paris for an online magazine."

"Ah, but that sounds so exciting! I sometimes think how I would like to acquire a computer and as you say, go "on line", though to tell the truth this is a bit overwhelming. Still, I might yet learn how to swim the internet!"

". . . *pardon*, Gabrielle. To "surf" the internet.

"*Ah, oui*," she laughs. "To surf then." She reaches in her bag and retrieves a treat for Joie who accepts it daintily. "And do you visit Paris alone?"

"Yes, alone," a waiter appears to fill my wine-glass, "I'm married. But my husband, Jon, remains in New York."

"Ah," is her only reply. Gabrielle asks nothing more about Jon, as an American might, an example of the famous French code of privacy that is kept for all but one's closest friends.

We talk about Paris. Gabrielle has lived here most of her adult life and speaks of its charms as though the city is a person.

She asks if I'm ready to order and recommends the steak tartar, preferring a filet of sole for herself. Appreciative of the privacy Gabrielle's allowed me, I'm careful with my own questions. But I manage to draw her out enough to learn that she came to Paris from a small village in the South as a young woman and worked as a secretary at an import company until she met and married Charles LaCroix, a junior diplomat. They moved from post to post, country to country, until returning to Paris toward the end of his illustrious career. He passed away some time ago but it's obvious that she adored him.

I order crème brulée for dessert. When it arrives I slowly crack its burnt crust with my spoon as Gabrielle sips her coffee. After only a couple of hours in her company I already know that there's something quite special about this woman and that I want very much to spend more time with her. Still, I don't want to presume on her generosity if, as Mitzi says, she rarely socializes these days. Then a sudden idea occurs to me and for once in my life, I act spontaneously on it.

"Gabrielle, were you really serious about wanting to learn how to use a computer?"

"*Bien sur*, but I..."

"Well. I'd be happy to help you choose one, set it up and show you how to use it."

She places her cup back in its saucer, "But, *non*, that is too generous, *cherie!*"

"It wouldn't take that much time."

"But the setting up as you call it, *c'est très difficile, non?*"

"No. *Non*. It's easy. And teaching you to use it

would be my pleasure. Honestly, it would be fun!"

"But," she pauses, shaking her head, "but here you come for the pleasure of Paris and then you would have this task to attend to…"

"Gabrielle, let me do this for you!" my insistence surprises me, "truly, I'd enjoy it."

"Well," she looks down at Joie, who stares back at her as though the two of them were conferring on the matter. "Well… and so then, I would like to accept your kind offer. But," she pauses dramatically enough to make me think of Mitzi, "only on the understanding that you allow me to do something for you in return."

"Well… sure."

"You will," her smile is wide and warm, "please allow me to properly introduce my city to you."

My heart skips a happy beat but I hesitate.

"It is a fair exchange, Suzanne. Will you not accept it?"

"Well… actually I would love that, Gabrielle. I accept!"

We reach, laughing, across the table to shake hands on our bargain.

And I have no idea what a life changing bargain it will be.

Looking back now, I believe the two of us were fated to meet.

A day rarely passes when Gabrielle doesn't come to mind—some wise or witty remark she made, the warmth of her infectious laughter, the pleasure of her charming company and all I received from it. She remains ever my guiding angel, oracle, and mentor, her life an example in the art of living and loving well.

From her I learned that kindness and graciousness are the foundation of true elegance and style, the honest expression of the best in us.

And under her graceful guidance, the transformation from Susan to Suzanne took place in my heart as well as my mirror.

Here then are the French lessons *ma chère* Gabrielle taught me...

Avril
April

L'Élégance
Elegance...

Gabrielle and I are out shopping one afternoon when she pauses before a small florist shop.

"*Regardez!*" she exclaims. Red rose petals are strewn along the sidewalk, piled high like scarlet snow drifts, on either side of the shop's entry. "*Elle sont très jolies.*"

"It is very pretty," I breathe in the scent of what must have been dozens of roses.

"*Maman* would have loved this. In spring and summer our home was filled with the flowers she grew in our garden. And in winter, if all we could afford was a single blossom, she would place it in the window, where our neighbors as well as our selves might enjoy it."

"Your mother sounds wonderful."

"*Oui. C'était une originale. Maman* attended to the small details of life that made it a pleasure to everyone else. And then too, there was about her such a loveliness of person. She remains for me the epitome of elegance."

We begin walking again, Joie tip tapping along between us.

I swing the shopping bag in my hand. "When I think of elegance, it seems like a rare quality that few women possess. Usually women with more time and money than I have."

Gabrielle stops beside the doorway of a *boucherie,*

picks Joie up and hands her to me. "Ah Suzanne," she smiles, "simply to live well, which is elegance at its most basic, is neither of those," she turns toward the door, "*L'elégance* is the manner in which one does a thing."

Joie and I wait out on the sidewalk watching through the window while Gabrielle confers with the butcher inside. The spicy, delicious smell from dozens of sausages of every shape and size hanging over the counter wafts through the open door. For Joie, this must be the equivalent of a whiff of Number Five outside the Chanel boutique.

Gabrielle concludes her business then steps back outside to join us. "Emile sends you this," she says, offering Joie a bite of meat which immediately disappears.

"Now here, *ma cherie*," she holds up a small square wrapped in butcher paper, its bright red string tied in a jaunty bow, "is a perfect example of elegance. Emile could have torn off the paper and just," she slaps the wrapper, "like so with some tape. But *non*, he wrapped the package as though it were a *cadeau*, a gift, a bit of red string instead of the boring brown sort," she laughs, "and not only a delicious chop! *C'est l'elégance!*"

"*Oui*," I snuggle Joie who continues to regard the little packet as more chop than work of art. We continue our walk.

"It's the manner in which you do a thing, anything, that gives it elegance. It doesn't have to be grand or cost a great deal of time and money. The simplest things give us the greatest pleasure—the rose petals on the pavement, the chop from the butcher! *Oui*, Joie?" she taps the dog lightly on the nose with the packet.

The art of elegance is one of the most valuable lessons I ever began to learn, from Gabrielle. I say began because its pursuit is an ongoing process for me. I will always be learning to choose more carefully how I do something—having dinner at the table instead of in front of the television; reapplying my lipstick after lunch; deciding fresh flowers aren't only for weddings and funerals. And what a pleasure each elegant choice is.

And as is often the case with the most elegant among us, I don't think Gabrielle ever guessed how perfectly she herself embodied the quality she so admired in her *maman*.

No more than the rose petals on a sunny sidewalk suspect how they charm us.

Or the single blossom in a window guesses how it warms our winter hearts.

La Joie de Vivre
The Joy of Living...

There's a tiny, charming creature very much a part of Gabrielle's life—her miniature dachshund, Joie. Like the lamb in the nursery rhyme, almost everywhere that Gabrielle goes, Joie goes as well, often tucked beneath an arm.

Since dogs and their owners often look alike, it's not surprising that Gabrielle and Joie are both small and sleek. But at times they also share an identical expression, an amiable look of pure pleasure on both their faces, which makes me laugh.

Joie is accepting of new people in her life, as long as Gabrielle introduces them properly. Then when meeting them a second time she is completely enthusiastic, tiny tail wagging her whole body.

"I've fallen in love with your dog," I say to Gabrielle. We watch Joie chase a low flying pigeon larger than she is. We're sitting on a wooden bench in the shade of an aged elm in the park across from her flat. Nearby is a small pond laden with lilies and beyond that a "lover's maze" of ivy-covered hedges, famed as a place for marriage proposals.

"I'll never forget the first time I saw her, in a pen full of her brothers and sisters. In the midst of all those squirming little bodies, Joie looked straight up at me with those brown eyes. Then she ran toward me as fast as her little legs could carry her, stumbling over the grass, claiming me as her own. She made the decision for both of us. Joie, Joie! *Viens ici, mon choux.*" Gabrielle dissolves into laughter. "Calling her is useless, you know. She is so determined to catch that bird, it does not even occur to her she won't."

"A big spirit in a small body," I say as Joie rushes back and forth, tilting at her own version of windmills, "Joie is the perfect name for her."

The pigeon flies away, Joie runs up to our bench and is immediately scooped up by Gabrielle.

"In some difficult times of my life she has been my teacher as well as my companion, *n'est-ce pas, mon chou chou?*" Gabrielle rubs the little head, smoothes the velvety ears.

A small boy with his mother enters the park. He's playing with a large red ball. Joie squirms to be put down. She runs and jumps after the ball as it bounces along, regarding it as her own. The boy, delighted runs after the ball and Joie.

The ball rolls into the pond a few yards away. An elderly, grey haired gardener working nearby picks up his rake and runs to retrieve it before boy and dog take a sudden bath.

Gabrielle and the boy's mother chorus grateful *merci's* to him, then nod to one another smiling as Joie and the boy begin their game again.

"To live with *joie de vivre*, as well as its namesake

Joie, is to live a constant adventure, to be ready for each day to bring us something new... whether it is an episode one prefers to experience, or not."

She pauses to watch ball, boy and Joie disappear down a tree-lined path. The mother follows them, after stopping briefly to accept the small bouquet of cuttings the gardener shyly offers her.

"A very wise friend of mine once said—sometimes you choose life, sometimes it chooses you. But you are the only one who can decide to be happy as you live it. To live it with *joie de vivre*, what other way could there be?"

Silently I gather up my things as we prepare to leave. Here in the park this afternoon, I suddenly realize that my body may have arrived in Paris some weeks ago, but my mind has remained in New York. I am still losing a great deal of the beautiful present in the confusing past.

Perhaps it's time for me to start chasing a bouncing ball of my own, not wasting a moment of what *is* now, for what *may* or may *not* be in my life later. This will take some practice on my part. Fortunately I have an excellent role model. Right now she is playing somewhere in this park with a large red ball.

Gabrielle and I link arms and walk together toward the shady path that Joie is intent on leading us down.

Le Cachet
Style...

Gabrielle seems particularly pleased when I ask her to join me on a visit to the *Musée de la Mode et du Textile* on the rue de Rivoli. "Not many visitors to Paris know of this place," she says, "and it's one of the more fascinating." We walk up the broad stairs that curve toward the entrance of the elegant white stone building.

"For me, no women in the world have such a sense of style as the French," I hand my ticket to the woman at the door. "Only yesterday I watched a woman probably in her late 70's, shopping. She had gorgeous snow white hair worn in a chignon, her makeup was perfect. She wore a simple dress with low heeled shoes. She was impeccable."

" *C'est vrai*, we have a history of style, *cachet* if you prefer. Did you know the first high heels were made for Catherine de Medici, when she married the Duc d'Orleans? Or that Louis the 14th was so vain of his legs that he wore five inch heels decorated with miniature battle scenes to show them off? Or that Marie Antoinette ascended the scaffold wearing two inch heels? "Gabrielle chuckles. "*C'est très mauvais*, it's very bad indeed, to lose one's head, but to have on the wrong shoes as one does so, that's unthinkable."

We walk slowly down an aisle of mannequins wearing 18th century costumes. "So, Gabrielle... how do you do it? Is it bred in the bloodlines to know the right height of heel or the perfect scarf?"

"*Oui. Et non.* I know you have a love affair with us, *ma chère*, and I adore you for it. But many women here don't know the rules of *cachet*."

"I bet the first is to have a huge bank account."

"*Non, pas du tout.* The most stylish female I ever knew, Caroline Dupris, who I knew when we were school girls, was the poorest girl in our class. She had but one dress to wear at a time, always passed down to her from one of her many older sisters. And yet, she was *toujours très soignée*, impeccably groomed, even when the rest of us were grubby. Occasionally she would receive a new ribbon or hair band. And she had either a sweater, carefully mended, or a coat, also a hand me down. This was her wardrobe. "

"How sad."

"*Mais non.* Caroline did the best with what she had and then seemed to think no more about it. At the age of twelve, this sweet girl possessed more *cachet* and natural confidence than women I know now who buy out the collections. Later in life, when as a young career woman I was barely surviving, I would remember Caroline and know I could put my best foot forward if my shoe was well polished if not the most stylish."

"Whatever happened to her?"

"That does not matter so much at just this moment, Suzanne. Caroline was—is—the answer to your question about style. To possess true *cachet* is to be confident enough not to simply mimic the current fashion, but to create one's own timeless look; to be impeccable whether one possesses a huge wardrobe or one dress; to give effort to one's appearance—but then to forget about it. In this way, you wear the clothes; the clothes do not wear you. As Madame Chanel said."

I laugh, "I never thought I'd hear a French woman recommend forgetting about her ensemble."

Gabrielle joins in my laughter. "You will hear it from this one, *mon amie*. As you Americans say 'life is too short!' But come along," she gently pushes me through the entrance to another room. Some of the richly embroidered dresses on display here are almost as wide as their wearers must have been tall. Gabrielle exclaims, "How did these women walk through a doorway, do you think and then, how to sit on a chair?"

An hour or more passes and we've thoroughly explored the museum. I walk toward the exit, but Gabrielle takes my arm and leads me in the opposite direction and down a hallway labeled *"privé."*

I allow myself to be led through several sets of doors until we come to one marked *"Directrice, Musée de la Mode et du Textile."*

A chic young receptionist at the desk just inside looks up inquiringly, then smiles at Gabrielle. *"Bon Jour, Madame LaCroix, Comment-allez vous?"*

"Bon Jour, Nicole. Très bien, merci. Nous sommes ici

pour voir La Directrice," says Gabrielle.

"*Bien sur, Madame,*" replies the woman. She rises and crosses the room to knock on the ornate double doors that face us.

Gabrielle turns to me, with a twinkle in her eye. "And now you shall find out what happened to Caroline," she says. "She will tell you all about it herself, over lunch."

L'Ordre
Order...

It's almost May, a beautiful morning and Gabrielle is on her way to pick me up at my flat. Today we will venture outside Paris to visit the remarkable *Chateau Vaux-le-Vicomte*, at Melun, a short train ride away. I'm fascinated by the story of this chateau built in the 1600's by Nicolas Fouquet, Louis XIV's Minister of Finance. History has it that at first sight of the chateau and its acres of gardens, fountains, and canals, Louie was so impressed he later modeled Versailles on it. And so enraged with a display of wealth rivaling his own, that he sent Monsieur Fouquet to jail the next day.

That jail cell must have been just about the size of this one room flat, I think looking around me now. But with much less clutter; clothes, papers and books filling it.

This is not a good day for Gabrielle to see my place for the first time, nor for me to have overslept. There's hardly time to dress much less straighten things, before she arrives.

Her knock sounds on the door and I open it to have my arms filled with glorious purple irises, their woody fragrance filling the air.

"I saw these and knew you had to have them for... ," Gabrielle looks around, ". . . your flat." Even her impeccable manners cannot mask a slight look of surprise—or is it horror—at what she sees.

"These are lovely. *Merci beaucoup*," I wonder how I will unearth a vase to put them in.

"I see that you are rearranging things this morning, *chérie*."

I'm embarrassed by what a mistress of understatement she is. "I apologize for the lack of order but it seems that wherever I am things are never in their place—at my office, in my home, even here. It drives Jon crazy. Actually it drives me crazy too."

"You say 'in their place' as though your books would toss themselves into the bookcase and your clothes scurry into the closet. They would do this when you are asleep perhaps?" she smiles.

"I'm glad one of us has a sense of humor about it."

Gabrielle puts the flowers in the sink. "*J'ai une bonne nouvelle pour toi*, Suzanne. The order you think is missing is present already."

"*Excuse-moi*. Order is here? I'm just not seeing it?"

"Order is always present, since it is the natural state of things. It is we who pile things on top of it, concealing it. This is confusing for the room. Here. You, put away the clothes while I do this," she begins making neat piles of papers covering the table next to my laptop.

"Confusing for the room?"

"Well, perhaps not for the room itself, but certainly, for whoever must live in it."

I think of poor Jon as I began to sort shirts and

scarves into drawers. He is one of those naturally neat people, who, had he been present, would now be throwing his arms around Gabrielle and hugging her. "Oh thank you," he would cry, "*merci.*"

"Ah, a dictionary," she says picking it up from the pile on the floor. "*Regarde ici.* Order. An organized state with elements arranged neatly and harmoniously.' "

"The harmony part sounds good." I retrieve a suede jacket from the back of a chair and hang it up, locate two and a half pairs of pumps, give up on the missing one and line them up in the bottom of a closet.

"It is more than good, *ma chère.* We feel harmonious when things are in their places, having arrived there," she laughs, "most often with our help."

We work quietly side by side for another half an hour or so, putting away, arranging. I notice first a sense of relief, then something close to pleasure, arises in me.

The charm of my room, its bay window looking into the little courtyard, reasserts itself, enhanced by a huge vase the concierge has lent us, now filled with the purple blue irises.

I wish I could say that when we leave for Melun this day, I also leave the practice of disarray behind. *Mais non*, it takes some real effort for me to change the habits of a lifetime.

But day by day I start to realize that it's just as easy to toss a scarf into a drawer as onto a chair; that the fascinating passage in a book will not be lost when it's returned to its shelf; that flowers dying in their vase will not revive themselves.

Slowly, very slowly, I learn that when I create order around me, a sense of harmony and peace begins to reside within me.

I am never going to train my dresses to hang themselves up anyway. They're just too stubborn for that.

L'empathie
Empathy...

Gabrielle and I both prefer the smaller museums of Paris, such as the *Musée de l'Orangerie* near the *Jardin des Tuileries*, to the gargantuan *Louvre*. *L'orangerie's* chief possession is an oval shaped room inlaid with huge panels of Monet's *Waterlilies*. We stand in the center of the room and turn slowly around looking at the continuous shadings of pearlescent pastels, water, lilies.

In the past I've come here and been deeply moved by all the beauty around me. Today however, is different. A single, errant tear slides down my cheek. I brush it away but not before Gabrielle has seen it. Silently she puts her arm through mine and leads me out of the museum and through the gardens outside, to a café in their midst.

We find a table and sit. After ordering tea, she looks at me, her eyes as serious as my own. "*Ma chère Suzanne, tu as la peine de coeur?*"

"*Oui.* I'm sick at heart."

"I don't wish to intrude. We will just sit here together and have our tea. But I am glad to listen if you care to speak about what troubles you."

"Well..." I embarrass myself, starting to cry in earnest now, fumbling in my bag for a Kleenex that is not there. "Jon and I had a terrific row on the phone this morning."

Gabrielle snaps open her purse, draws out the soft cotton handkerchief that is always there and hands it to me.

Gratefully I make use of it to compose myself. "Gabrielle," I pause, "There's something I haven't told you. I'm not just here to enjoy Paris and write. I also came because I thought that being away from Jon for a while would give me some perspective on our marriage, which, actually, has some real problems. Jon didn't want me to come, but I felt I had to. What I hadn't counted on was how much I miss him. So this morning I called him in New York, to ask if he'd take some time off from his job, come over for a while... ,"she sits still, listening. "It was wonderful to hear his voice again and he sounded so happy to hear from me but... but he won't come over. He says that now he agrees with me, that we need time away from each other." Suddenly I'm more angry than sad, "He didn't want me to go away so now he's punishing me for it, refusing to come." Our tea arrives and is set before us.

When the waiter is gone Gabrielle reaches out to take my hand in hers.

"Suzanne, let me ask you something. What if Jon doesn't wish to punish you, but is sincere... that he agrees with you about having this time apart?"

"Things are never that simple with us, Gabrielle."

She squeezes my hand, releases it, picks up her cup of tea. "*Non, le marriage n'est jamais simple, c'est vrai.*

But why don't you give him, and yourself, the benefit of believing him about this?"

"Because..." I can't seem to finish the sentence.

"Because... because it is easier to be angry than to be hurt?"

She takes a sip of tea, sets the flowered china cup carefully down on its saucer. "Suzanne, do you know the meaning of the word *empathie* ?"

"Of course... I mean I know what the dictionary says."

"*Empathie* is to put one's self in another's place, to respect the other's feelings, even if—sometimes especially if—they don't agree with ours, so that we begin to understand..."

I interrupt, "That's a lovely sentiment Gabrielle, but Jon and I couldn't understand each other any less than we do right now."

She brushes away a leaf that has fallen on the table, looks up at me. "Tell me, Suzanne, is it your hope that things will change for Jon and you while you are here, change for the good?"

"Of course I'd like things to get better. And I'm here to figure out how. . . "

"You can do all the 'figuring out' as you say, that you want, *cherie*. But if you want to stay together, one of you has to do something to begin a new understanding between you. If you are not willing to feel some *empathie* for your husband, how can this begin?"

I pick up, then set my cup down. "It's not fair that I have to be the one. . ."

"Oh fair, fair, fair. Love is not fair." She is stern.

"So, if I were to begin to have more empathy with Jon I would just start to believe him? Whatever he says?"

"*Non*, not just blindly believe, Suzanne. I do not suggest you to be the fool. But if you would at least try to understand what he feels. You say he didn't want you to leave him in New York... then only think how difficult it must be for him to stay away from you."

I resist what Gabrielle is saying. Then grudgingly allow myself to consider it. And then something I've never thought of occurs to me. What would it have been like for *me* to be the one left behind? How angry would I have been? How hurt and afraid?

She speaks, "Suzanne, we put ourselves in another's place because that's what love does. Love seeks to understand the beloved for his or her own sake. And from this *empathie* for the other, comes *la confiance*, a deeper trust between us. Without it we don't have a real marriage, we have but a contract to live together."

I move my chair further into the shade of the enormous oak beside us. "You make it all sound so easy, Gabrielle."

"Do I? Nothing could be harder, especially in the beginning. To try to understand another's reasoning instead of simply following one's own? *C'est du travail*. For me it was especially difficult." She brings her chair closer to mine. "Charles taught me much about this, actually. As a diplomat he had always to be able to see another's point of view. At times it was truly dangerous for him, as well as for many others, if he could not create *empathie* between people."

She pauses, "*En plus*, Suzanne, That still doesn't mean it was easy. I found it most challenging at first to say to Charles, that on some occasions, he was right and I was wrong." She suddenly laughs at the surprise on my face. "*Oui, oui, c'est amusant.* When we see how like children we can be, refusing to yield our corner of *le bac à sable.*"

I can't help but smile at the image of myself and Jon, as two-year olds, squaring off across a sandbox, neither of us willing to give an inch.

What Gabrielle is saying makes more rather than less sense, whether it's easy to agree with or not.

I know this decision I've made to be apart from Jon is the right one for me. So why wouldn't I allow it to be the right one for him? I owe him and us that much. No matter how much I miss him.

A sense of peace begins to descend in me as my glance strays toward the majestic fountains of the *Tuileries.* Rainbows chase the sun through the cascading drops. Like the colors the heart chases through the rain.

I turn back toward Gabrielle, "I think I will probably be making another phone call in a few hours."
She nods, "*Ah, oui?*"

"This one will be to let Jon and myself off the emotional hook I was putting us on."

"*Empathie*, Suzanne?"

"*Oui*, Gabrielle, a little empathy. For the man I love."

"He loves you too, Suzanne," her green eyes shine, "And that's enough for now. *N'est-ce pas, cherie?*"

"*Oui*, Gabrielle," I turn to look once more at the rainbows shining through the tumbling waters, "That's enough for now."

Le moins vaut plus
Less is more...

Whether it's the amount of jewelry one wears, the size of dessert one consumes or the point at which one controls instead of contributes to a conversation—less of a thing always makes it more valuable. And *none* is better than too much!

L'indépendence
Independence...

If romantically involved, devote yourself to being madly in love, but keep in mind that finding love is no excuse for losing oneself.

Maintain your own style, your own mind, your own assets—and opinions.

Always be faithful—first to yourself! Then to your beloved.

Pas de Regrets
No regrets...

Regret nothing! Not the chocolate croissant you put in your mouth this morning, nor any word that may have issued from that same mouth.

If there is a way to admit or make right, a wrong you have done someone, bravely do so—and immediately! Then learn what you can from the experience and move on.

You are a human being, who *must* occasionally err—not a perfect angel—nor the bore that perfect angels can sometimes be!

Mai
May

L'Amour-Propre
Self Esteem...

The dozens of small, neighborhood movie houses all over Paris that show classic American movies are a charming surprise for me. What a treat it is to walk into one of these tiny theaters, seating as few as thirty people and see everything from Preston Sturgis classics to Joan Crawford in all her glory.

On a Sunday afternoon, I take Gabrielle to see *Sweet Bird of Youth*, one of my favorites. Paul Newman is Chance Wayne, an aging pretty boy still trying to make it in Hollywood and Geraldine Page plays Alexandra del Lago, a movie star past her prime.

Afterward as we walk down the street, Gabrielle grows eloquent on both the film and Paul Newman's blue eyes. "He not only is a most beautiful man," she announces, "but a master at his craft."

Suddenly she stops to peer into the window of a hat shop, pointing out a confection that one does not wear so much as place atop one's head.

"But," she says thoughtfully, as we continue on, "as much as I adored Paul, Geraldine gave the most brilliant speech in the film. And it had only three words."

"What was that?

"It was toward the end of the film. Chance tries to frighten Alexandra. He grabs her by her wrists and makes her look at herself in the mirror, in all disarray.

He yells at her, 'Tell me! What do you see there? What?'"

We stop on the sidewalk "Now I remember..."

"And Alexandra, triumphant, looks into the mirror, and says, 'I. See. Me.' Three words, the best thing in the film." Gabrielle links her arm through mine and begins to walk again.

"Because?"

"In three words, she perfectly expresses the meaning of '*l'amour-propre*'"

"*L'amour-propre?*"

"Self esteem. She looks into the mirror and sees herself for herself. *Oui*, she knows she can be *un vrai monstre*. She knows she is older, a terrible thing for a film star. And that she relies too much on the gigolos and the cocktails. She knows herself to be imperfect *mais magnifique*. And she loves who she sees in spite of who she sees. And as a woman who accepts and triumphs in herself, nothing, no-one can shake her faith in herself. *Ça, ç'est l'amour-propre. Très simple.*"

Gabrielle turns and leads me back toward the hat shop to peer in the window again. We will no doubt, return tomorrow when it's open. She'll try that bit of fluff on, decide in its favor or not. And I will receive a quick lesson on which hats make me look my most "*séduissante.*"

Her quick lesson in *amour-propre* comes to mind the next morning as I step from the bath and glimpse a full view of my body, something I usually avoid. Then I remember Alexandra Del Lago looking into her mirror, so fearlessly. I stop myself from turning away and look at my body and myself in the eye. I see the stomach that's never been truly flat, the extra pounds I've gained and lost dozens of times.

I take a breath. Slowly I run my gaze over the flesh, muscles and yes, the fat that have gotten me through nearly forty summers and winters, through heartbreak and exhaustion, through a brush with cancer. I admire the strong legs that keep me standing, the arms that reach out to embrace a friend, the torso that still stretches sensually in most directions. This is the real, not airbrushed body of a forty, not a twenty year old. And my life is a real, not airbrushed life.

I smile at me in the mirror.

Here I am in Paris, a "woman of a certain age" with the accumulated wisdom of my years, and the body that got her here. I think I will take this body out for a walk and buy it a silly hat or a flower or a croissant.

I. See. Me. And I like what I see.

Le Charme et Le Charisme
Charm and Charisma...

On a spring morning, Gabrielle and I approach number 30 rue de Paradis, the museum and showroom of Baccarat, here since 1892. She has assured me I "shall see the most fabulous display of crystal in Paris," while she chooses a present for her niece's wedding.

As we open the door a young saleswoman looks up and asks how she might be of service. Her gaze, plainly displeased, lingers on Joie who smiles up at her from beneath Gabrielle's arm.

Her frown remains fixed as Gabrielle assures her that Joie will disturb nothing. But from past experience, I know it's just a matter of time until its direction will reverse itself. I wander through Baccarat's magical rooms, amazed at the splendor glittering down every aisle, from the most gigantic chandelier I've ever seen to a sculpted princess whose crown, hair and dress are all made of crystal.

It doesn't surprise me when I return to the front of the store to find Gabrielle and the saleswoman Chloé, deep in conversation while Joie dines on a bit of pate from a plate on Chloé's desk.

Chloé then guides us around the store, unlocking private rooms, revealing treasures most visitors never glimpse. By the time we depart, delighted with our special tour and the perfect wedding present, an exquisite crystal bowl etched with flowers, Chloé is as pleased with our visit as we are.

As we walk toward the bistro she's chosen for lunch, I take Joie from her arms, hug her to me and look at Gabrielle happily strolling beside me. "Everywhere we go, no matter who we meet, you seem to make friends with them so easily. Infact it seems," I smile, "as though you have almost cast a spell on them."

"*Mais non*, it is they who fascinate me, *cherie. Chaque personne qu'on rencontre est très interessante, très unique.* Every person is so unique, each like a novel to be read for the first time. Each is quite amazing really."

We enter the *Café des Muguets*, already filled for lunch. Henri, a rotund Frenchman straight out of central casting, greets Gabrielle effusively, kissing her the requisite three times. The best table in the house materializes as he announces he must personally select what we dine on and drink, to be certain it meets the standards he requires for Madame.

He disappears amid a flurry of waiters who begin to circle our table like attentive blackbirds.

"Again! You see?" I laugh. "It's not just that you enjoy people and their stories. You seem to charm them somehow. How do you do it?"

"Charm is nothing I think of myself as having," she is plainly mystified. "nor anything I think of doing, Suzanne."

I don't give up, "Gabrielle, you may not think of

yourself as charming, but you must have known others who you thought of as charming or charismatic—someone you learned this way of being from?"

Gabrielle shrugs, looks off into space, then smiles. *"Ma chère maman était certainement charmante. Maman* was the very first person in my life whom I experienced as charming, before I even knew the word. *C'est vrai.* And now as I think of it, infact how could I have forgotten?" her green eyes fasten on a memory, "it was from her that I first heard the word. *Oui, oui,* when I was quite young, I recall her speaking of both charm and charisma, and the difference in them, in the form of a little fable."

A waiter appears with two aperitifs courtesy of Henri.

"As a young girl, I had fallen beneath the spell of *Maman's* sister, my charismatic *Tante* Eugénie, an actress. *Maman* noticed this and said nothing about my infatuation, except to tell me this tale." She pauses, "If it will not bore you..."

"Sil vous plait..."

"Ah... so, it went something like this. There once was a very beautiful young goddess named Grace. She was the daughter of Sophia, the all powerful goddess of Wisdom. Grace fell in love with Eros and soon gave birth to a set of exquisite twin girls, Charm and Charisma.

The twins were at once admired and adored by all

those they encountered. But Sophia noticed that while Grace loved both equally, Charisma demanded and received the greater share of attention. Charm, quieter and more subtle, required less and so was given less. Sophia took Grace aside one day and said 'Remember my darling daughter, the fire that burns brightest is not always the longest lasting, nor is it the greater gift.

Charisma has her own precious purpose, to inflame others with her birthright of inspiration, imagination and vivid emotion. She is the muse of the great masters and artists and as they are, so is she fascinating and self centered. Charisma is the flame of aliveness that humans will always yearn for and aspire to.

Charm is not so much the flame, as the glowing embers around it, the gentle radiance that warms gods and mortals alike through many seasons. Hers is a quieter way than Charisma's. But she is loyal and true to her own purpose, to rejoice in the moment at hand and to see in each being she encounters, something precious and unique. Mortals treasure this in her for they are drawn to her joy and quiet peace, her acceptance of them as whatever they are.

Prepare Charisma, if you can as a mother, to learn the wisdom of becoming more like Charm as she grows older—*le centre de la chambre pour le centre du Coeur...* to surrender the center of the room, for the center of the heart.

And never forget that Charm and Charisma are

both gifts of the Gods, through Grace and Eros, to all mortals.'"

I look down to see our first course already before me.

"What a beautiful story, Gabrielle. *Merci.* And it doesn't surprise me that your *maman* was your first encounter with charm and its lessons. As she was with elegance." I lift a spoon of vichyssoise to my lips. The subtle taste of chilled potatoes and leeks is delicious. "But, whatever happened to Eugénie?"

"She was for many years a great star of the *Théatre des Française*, famed not only for her acting abilities but for her volatility and passion. She lifted and broke many hearts. Much later she retired to live quietly near the *Bois de Boulogne.* She left behind the stage and all the glory it had brought her. But she seemed happier in her later years, just to be teaching a few students, the actors and stars to come, until she passed away. She seemed more… at peace." She pauses, "And it's funny now I think of it, but..."

"*Quoi?*"

"Though Eugénie outlived her by many years, I noticed something before *Maman* died. The two of them had come to look more and more alike as they aged. More like twins than sisters."

A vintage champagne arrives at our table. We watch respectfully as the waiter makes a ceremony of uncorking it, pouring a taste for Gabrielle, then filling each of our flutes.

"A toast," I hold up my glass, "to charm and charisma, the true twins of grace and eros."

Oui!" cries Gabrielle, touching her glass to mine,
"*et vive Maman! Vive Eugénie!*"

Les Vacances de Douze Heures
The Twelve-Hour Vacation...

We're strolling through the *Petit Palais* on a beautiful May morning, enjoying the building as well as an exhibition of Rousseau's paintings. The *Grand* and *Petite Palais* were built for the 1900 Paris Exposition, the same one for which the *Eiffel Tower* was erected and both are masterpieces of soaring glass, steel and stone in the art nouveau style.

Gabrielle announces she will soon take a holiday. "*Oui,*" she says, "I have been very busy. Last weekend was the marriage of my favorite niece then there was the repainting of my flat. And my dear friend Caron required some time and care from me. *Je suis très fatiguée et je vais prendre des vacance.*"

I reach out to relieve her of Joie, who grins up at me and wags her tail. "Where will you go on your vacation? How long will you be away?"

"To a most luxurious retreat. And I shall be away for twelve hours."

"Only twelve hours? I thought you were really going somewhere."

"*Bien sur* I am going somewhere—*directement à ma chambre.*"

"To your room?"

She reaches out to tickle Joie's ear, "Many years

ago when my life was much busier than it is now I realized I was completely exhausted, not only in body and but in soul. But in that time of my life, I had not the time nor the money for *des vacances traditionnels*. Then it occurred to me that if I couldn't travel to some exotic destination, I could at least get away from the world and its cares for a few hours. So *voila*, I invented les *"Vacances de Douze Heures."*

We pause to look at a painting of a woman reclining on a couch in the midst of a lush green landscape filled with plants and fanciful flowers. The colors and textures are so rich, we stand mesmerized for a while.

I break the silence, "But, a vacation that only lasts for twelve hours?"

"Oui, Cherie. Twelve hours is enough when you cut yourself completely off from the world. You turn off the phone, the doorbell, television, radio, anything that requires your attention. For you this would include the computer as well," she smiles. "You close your bedroom door, you get into your bed. You may depart on your vacation at any time you please, but having done so, you may do only three things—sleep, relax or read. For twelve hours."

"That's all you do? Stay in bed for twelve hours?"

"Oui! Très simple, non? Even now when my life is so much quieter, I remind myself to take this little holiday at least once a month, abandoning those few obligations that fill my time. Many of my friends follow this

regime as well. They tell me they feel they've been away to a spa in Switzerland for a week, instead of twelve hours. They are revitalized. *Complètement!*"

"That sounds lovely. But at the moment I don't really need it, I'm sort of on a four month vacation..."

" *C'est vrai,*" she says, "*mais souviens-toi ce qu'on dit en France...*'

"What do the French say?"

"How lovely to do nothing all day, and then to rest afterwards."

I examine the last painting in the exhibit. A man, wearing a suit, sits in a throne-like chair in jungle-like surroundings. Despite the palm trees behind him and the lush green grass beneath his feet, he doesn't relax in the chair so much as stiffly occupy it. I imagine that this is a man who even in the most exotic place has an agenda he sticks to every single day of his life.

Kind of like me I think, mentally running down my own list of things that must be done every day, even in Paris. I've always been proud of being a very responsible person. ("A little too responsible," Jon used to kid me.) I've also wished I could "get better" at relaxing, something that hasn't happened yet.

I take one last glance at the stiff man in his stiff chair, "Well... perhaps when you take your *vacances*, I might try one of my own. Just to see what it's like."

Gabrielle laughs and reaches out to take Joie back into her arms, "Having a vacation during your vacation! But only see how French you are becoming already?"

La Curiosité
Curiosity...

I'm nervous as I call for Gabrielle at her flat in
St. Germaine-des-Près this evening. She's invited me to
accompany her to an elegant dinner party given by an
old friend. As I stand waiting in the tiny blue foyer, she
tucks the ever present hanky into a small rose shaped
satin evening bag, gives a quick glance in the mirror and
says *"Cherie,* we are a bit early and I prefer not to surprise my hostess. Shall we have a Lillet before we go?"

I'm happy about any delay in leaving. Perhaps the
Lillet will make me a bit more confident? She leads
me into her small salon where French doors open out
toward the park across the street and gestures for me to
sit as she pours our sherry.

"Tell me more about tonight's dinner."

"You will like the Countess very much. She is quite
elderly, one of the honored fixtures of Parisian society.
And her sense of humor is as bright as her rouge. She
is known not only for assembling groups of interesting
people but for her magnificent food. Be prepared for at
least six courses and pace your wine accordingly."

"It sounds like a fascinating evening." I accept the
crystal sherry glass. "But to tell you the truth... I'm feeling as though I'm a bit out of my league."

"Out of your?"

"Formal six course dinners aren't exactly routine

for me. Oh, I know the trick about working my way in silver wise, so I probably won't embarrass myself too much there, but my French isn't that great and... well, I've never been to dinner with a countess before, so what will I say to whoever..."

"*Cherie*, take a sip of Lillet and a breath. You speak more than enough French and what you have no words for, your charm will convey. And it is not so much the proper fork or the perfect word, but a gracious attitude that's important, whether one is dining with a countess or a gendarme."

I take a gulp, not a sip, of sherry. "Gabrielle, to be honest it's not just tonight. I'm actually not comfortable in social gatherings with a lot of strangers. I hate it when I have to attend something for Jon's work and the room is full of people I don't know. You can't imagine all the miserable evenings I've endured and the fights we've had at the end of them."

She comes to sit on the couch beside me, quiet for a moment, then gently touches my arm. "Ah, but I can imagine them... perfectly."

Joie comes scampering into the room, is picked up and hugged then settles between us.

"Suzanne sometimes you remind me so much of myself it's like looking into a mirror, though a much younger one," she smiles. "When you speak of how it is with you now, I remember my first days as an embassy wife. *Oh, la, la... ce n'était pas facile.* To have to be with large groups of people was bad enough but I was also expected to become a sort of diplomat myself, making friends, creating social alliances."

Joie already asleep and dreaming moves her paws. "I used to be ill all day before an event, sometimes sick to the stomach."

"It actually made you sick?"

"It did for a while. As soon as I knew the date of an event I would begin to dread it. And when it was past I was relieved only until the next one. And this went on for some long time. Until I stumbled onto a very simple secret that changed everything for me."

I set my empty glass aside and sit forward listening.

"I came to understand, through much effort I assure you, that one thing is always certain. Whether one is in Paris, New York or Stalingrad hardly a person exists who doesn't adore talking about his or her self. In any social situation, the secret to being comfortable and at ease is to be curious."

"Curious?" Joie whines softly in her sleep.

"*Oui!* To be sincerely curious about another person, to find out how they came to be where they are either for this evening or in this life, this is a most absorbing pastime. And it allows us to forget about ourselves and the impression we make on someone else."

She chuckles, "And what's amusing is that after a person has spent some time talking to you all about herself, she will often regard you as a most fascinating person indeed.'"

She places our glasses on a silver tray. "Discovering curiosity was like stumbling onto a treasure map. With it I could make my way through an evening feeling much more self assured, feeling safe. And at some point, I don't know when, I started to actually enjoy myself."

Gabrielle's words make enough sense to slightly loosen the knot in my stomach. Just be curious, wonder about someone else, "wonder out loud" I guess. And that might make me seem interesting to them as well? That would be a welcome miracle.

She looks at her watch. "Ah! A few minutes and one is early, a few and one is late. *Nous ne voulons pas faire attendre la Contesse. Allons-y.*"

I remain seated. Gabrielle stops, smiles patiently, puts her hands on her hips. "Suzanne, I have for you *une petite tache ce soir*, an assignment for you tonight. At the evening's end, you will tell me the stories of three people you met. *C'est très facile.* I shall want to hear all about these fascinating people. You will do this? *Oui?*"

I take a breath and reluctantly stand up, "*Oui*, Gabrielle." There seems to be no other reply possible.

Later this evening in the dining room of a magnificent apartment located on the *Ile St.-Louis*, I try not to stare at the luxurious surroundings; the long, flower festooned table; the multiple mirrors that reflect glittering silver and crystal; the ornate ceilings inlaid with

18th century paintings.

We are on the fourth course, a salad of endive and raspberries, served with an excellent *Côte du Rhône* and I am mentally reviewing Gabrielle's assignment.

Earlier during cocktails, I've managed to make the acquaintance of Elise. I'd been afraid I might be asking her too many questions but she seemed pleased to talk all about the store she's set to open, selling handbags, *"le plus luxe de Paris."*

Now sitting on my left is an older diplomat, Etienne, with a hearing problem. He's a bit crotchety but seems to enjoy talking about his tour of duty in Thailand. His stories are so fascinating that I've already decided to go there someday.

On my right is a handsome thirty-something painter, D'Anton. He's been telling me all about a show of his new work opening next week. And now I find myself in a spirited discussion with him about Picasso, whom he's just announced is "the only truly important painter in modern art."

"But why would you say that? Picasso made his contributions, yes, but what about Miro, Leger, and all the others? And then later, people like Rothko and Pollock?" For a moment I've forgotten my shyness. I look up to meet the amused gaze of Gabrielle seated down the table from me. She sends me a wink so subtle I might have imagined it before turning back to her dinner partner.

In the midst of this new territory called curiosity, I'm still a bit nervous, feeling my way carefully along a winding path of questions and answers. And I don't expect ever to morph into a social butterfly.

But I'm beginning to understand that whether we meet them at a dinner party or at a bus stop each person we encounter has a story, often a fascinating one, which they're more than willing to tell. And how we by just being curious, can relax and listen forgetting all about our own shyness.

A butler leans to my left to remove the salad plate as D'anton interrupts my reverie. "What you say may be right, Suzanne," he lifts his glass of wine toward me in a toast, "but let's change the subject for a moment. Before you win the argument," he laughs. "I want to hear more about you and how you came to be in Paris. And tell me also," he grins and looks into my eyes, "for how long will you be staying?"

Oui, curiosity can be fun!

La Paresse

Laziness...

I've been around Gabrielle for some time before I notice one of her more subtle characteristics. Although often animated in conversation, there is about her a pronounced physical stillness. I never see her fidget, much less jiggle a leg or foot as I often catch myself doing. This creates an aura of calm about her that's as refreshing as it is attractive.

We're sitting at a table at *Ladurée* one afternoon, awaiting the arrival of some of their famous cakes when I remark on this. She laughs softy, leans toward me in a confiding way and says, "I'm glad you enjoy my... stillness as you call it?" She almost whispers, "But I am just being *paresseuse.*"

"You're being lazy?"

"*Mais oui.* That's what Madame Grenier called it anyway. She was the dancing teacher I was sent to the year I turned thirteen."

"I didn't know you studied dance."

"Well... only for a little while actually. To dance wasn't the true reason *Maman* sent me to her. *Non, Maman* had observed my changing body and how ill at ease I was with it, it seemed I fell over more chairs than I sat in."

"Most thirteen year old girls most go through something like that..."

"*C'est vrai*, but *Maman* did not like to see me suffering in this way, so she sent me to Madame Grenier. On my first visit, Madame sat me down in her salon, served me a cake and asked about my interests. I was chattering away when she interrupted me. 'Be still, Gabrielle." She added, 'Now, please continue without shaking your leg.' I resumed my story and my cake. In a moment or so, she said, 'You are tapping your foot Gabrielle. Put down your cake and listen.' Reluctantly I placed my plate on the table. 'Now what we must first do' Madame said, "is to teach you how to be still.'

'But I don't like to be still, Madame. It's… boring.'

'Yes. Being still *is* boring. But how do you like being lazy?'

'Very much, but *Maman* doesn't allow it too often.'

'She will allow this sort of laziness, I assure you. Now! Here is what you will do.'

"Madame knew from *Maman* how I adored reading. So, I was ordered to sit and read a favorite book each day. I was honor bound to stop reading as soon as I noticed myself fidgeting. I then must relinquish my book for the reminder of the day."

"And you always put the book right down?"

"*Non*, not always. But in time Madame's purpose was served. I began to grow tired of all my wriggling about, then began to like just being still, lazing about."

"And this made you feel more comfortable with yourself?"

"Well...this was but the first of many lessons Madame taught me, but *oui*, I recall being less self conscious," she chuckles, "and much less accident prone."

A plate of ivory colored iced cakes, topped by lacy sugared violets, arrives along with a pot of tea. "Then later, when boys came along, I began to see how being still when the other girls jumped about like monkeys had its advantages."

"You were a *femme fatale!*"

"*Pas fatale, non*...," she grins, "very far from that." Gabrielle picks up the teapot and pours tea into the paper thin china cups. "You know Suzanne, I've not thought of Madame Grenier in years... but what she taught me is quite true, it is so much more pleasant, simply easier to be still... to be lazy. "

She offers me the cakes before taking one for herself. And I become aware that beneath the table my toes are gently bopping to their own beat. How very American of me to never be still, even on a four month vacation. I still my foot, telling it somewhat impatiently, "relax." Right.

We continue our conversation, enjoying each other's company and the cakes a while longer. But now I realize I'm "having my cake and fidgeting too," eating with one hand while tapping my finger on the table top with the other.

I take a breath. I concentrate on the sugary bliss of the violets and icing as they melt in my mouth. After finishing the last delicious morsel, I sigh and sip my tea. I notice how quiet my body has become. Could it be that I am practicing laziness, a bit of Parisian *paresse*? Because for the moment anyway, I feel *almost* as relaxed and still as my friend looks, sitting in her warm silence across the table from me.

Le Panache
Panache...

Is style with a kick to it, a fillip of something just daring enough to almost cross the invisible boundary of good taste. Panache takes many forms—the little red feather on the toe of a black pump; a formal birthday dinner with silly hats at each place; the spontaneous call to a new acquaintance—"We must lunch together and today! Meet me at 1!"

La Voix
The Voice...

Be as conscious of your voice as you are of any other aspect you present to the world.

Be mindful of the manner in which you use it and of its pitch and volume.

The voice is one of the most charming calling cards a woman possesses. When age, wrinkles and an extra pound or two have arrived, the voice reminds us and others, of who we still are, of what our soul sounds like.

Cessez de Répéter
Cease repeating yourself...

In conversation, do not restate a point you've made, no matter how brilliant you may think it. For each repetition, there is a diminishing return for both speaker and listener.

Le Sourire
The Smile...

Why wouldn't you? It costs one nothing and its' immediately effect adds light to the world, whether it is returned or not.

And when it *is* returned, even between two strangers passing in the street, a smile serves its original purpose most perfectly—to create a brief spark of human connection.

Juin
June

Creativity
Créativité...

On a lazy afternoon we browse through one of Paris' many "*marché aux puces*" or flea markets, this one on the rue du Poteau, near Montmartre.

Each of these markets has a personality of its own. Some are known for food, others for rare books or antiques and some like this one for an eclectic mix of rare finds and pure junk.

At a large table Gabrielle works her way through a tub of gaudy beads, examining them with the patience of a jeweler searching for diamonds. In my arms Joie wiggles restlessly, sniffing the spicy aroma of roasting lamb wafting from a nearby Moroccan kiosk.

Gabrielle pulls out a strand of bright green beads shaped like scarabs then as is expected, bargains ferociously with the dealer. Her treasure safe in a plastic bag, we continue on.

"These will be perfect for the Egyptian motif of the new pot I am making."

"I didn't know you made pottery."

"Only for a brief time... a few months ago I met someone very gifted who also teaches. He is wonderful, very patient, which is needed with me. Pottery is so different from painting."

"You paint as well?"

"Less now since my romance with pots began,

but sometimes I pick up a brush." She reaches out to retrieve Joie who looks back longingly over her shoulder toward the roasting lamb.

Leaving the *marché*, we enter a rabbit warren of small streets then arrive at one of Paris' pocket-handkerchief-sized parks. This one is especially charming, its iron gate decorated with cherubs, while more cherubs frolic around the center of a small fountain.

A bench in the shade of a huge, leafy oak tree is empty and we claim it for a picnic. Joie is released to explore her new surroundings and the two of us begin to unpack the straw bag that holds our lunch.

"I envy your creativity, Gabrielle." I spread a red checkered cloth on the bench between us. "Most people don't have time for it."

She takes a demi of red wine and a small corkscrew from the bag, "Have the time, or make the time?"

"Maybe both. When I was writing copy in my old job I was so tired at the end of the day, the last thing I wanted was to write anything else," I watch Joie decide whether a large white poodle is friend or foe, "but now that I have all the time in the world I never get past the thinking stage on the play I keep wanting to write."

"You know," Gabrielle inserts a corkscrew and twists it slowly, "I truly believe that creativity is not the luxury we regard it to be, but a necessity for us to be truly happy with ourselves."

"'Necessity' is too close to 'duty' for me… one of

those 'should' words." I unwrap cheese and paté, arrange them on a plate.

"But having a good meal or seeing one's friends... these are necessities, *n'est-ce pas?*" Gabrielle removes wine glasses from their napkins, "things we make the time and effort for?"

"But we do them because they're a pleasure not an effort," I reply, tearing a crusty, still warm baguette in two.

"And yet Suzanne," she hands me a glass and pours wine into it, "you have said, more than once how important writing is to you in your life." She pours wine for herself and touches her glass to mine.

"I guess I think of writing as a passion and passion is spontaneous, it just happens or doesn't. You can't plan it."

Gabrielle tears a small piece from the baguette. "Ah, Suzanne, but you have made the perfect example!" She smears the bread with paté. "Do you remember when you and Jon first met... when you fell in love?"

"*Bien sur,*" I take a sip of wine. It tastes like ripe red berries.

"And when you became lovers did you see one another by accident? Only hope to run into him somewhere on the streets of New York?"

" No of course not." One of those crazy days in which Jon and I didn't even have time to meet for coffee comes to mind. But we had time he'd said, "to meet for a kiss." Between meetings I'd taxied to a certain corner on Madison Avenue and with the meter running leapt out of the cab and into his waiting arms before jumping back inside and speeding off again.

"Well your muse, the voice of your creativity is the same way. When she first called to you and you answered, it was a bit like falling in love, *non?*"

"*Oui*, in the beginning anyway… Gabrielle, I know where this is going. You're going to say one has to make a date and show up to write or paint or whatever just like for any other lover!*"

"*Précisément!* See how wise about this you are already?"

"It's one thing to know it and another to do it."

"So think, *cherie!* Where are you right at this moment, in this most precious time of your life? Are you not in Paris, the most magical city in the world, *la ville de l'amour?* What better place could there be to start an affair with your muse?"

She pops the bite of bread and paté into her mouth and allows a tiny "hmm" of pleasure to escape.

I try a bit of buttery *Tomme de Pyrénées.*

Gabrielle swirling the wine in her glass, says nothing more. Part of her genius is not to press a point made in conversation, particularly a point she has won.

We finish our picnic in friendly silence, watching Joie and her new friend chase each other around the fountain.

But something in me asks, quietly, almost sadly, when *will* I write that play or that book... do what I've dreamed about for so long?

If not here, where?

If not now, when?

Amour Toujours
Love Always...

In the heart of *St.-Germain-des-Près*, a most charming part of Paris, a deep stillness descends on summer Saturday afternoons. Down silent blocks and empty streets, in the midst of small parks, fountains murmur to themselves as flowers nod sleepily in the heat.

It's just such an afternoon, when feeling too lazy to move, I linger in Gabrielle's flat after lunch. I've been reading to her from the play I've begun to write. But now we sit silently in her small salon, enjoying the breeze from the French doors open to the park.

I study the painting of Charles LaCroix hanging in its place of honor above the marble fireplace.

"It's such a wonderful portrait of my darling... always he is here, keeping me company," Gabrielle says smiling up at him. "We were blessed with thirty years. I would have wished for thirty more."

"It sounds perfect."

She picks up a piece of needlepoint. "It wasn't, *bein sur*, involving as it did, two human beings. Many times especially during the first decade or so," she smiles, "we would have the most terrible quarrel and I would wonder if we could last through the night."

"What was the worst one you ever had?"

"Ah, but there were so many 'worst ones.'" She

laughs. "The same thing that attracted us to each other, a sense of independence, was the cause of many differences. I recall an especially silly row about what music to play for a dinner party. It only ended when our guests knocked on the door. At which time we compromised and played Brahms."

"Did you quarrel all the time?" I see Jon and me facing off across the living room, the bedroom, the kitchen.

She takes a stitch, then another, "Actually, a great secret of our happiness was when we, as you Americans say, decided to 'agree to disagree.'

"But the scenes, the quarrels like you were talking about," From the floor beside me Joie looks up, one ear flopped rakishly back. I can't help but smile and put her in my lap.

"Charles and I decided to avoid many of these scenes by expecting to be different from each other, accepting that we couldn't agree on all things. Instead of trying continually to change one another to our own way of thinking. Or doing."

"So. After you 'decided' this, you lived happily ever after?" Joie wiggles to be put down, trots over to her mistress.

She shakes her head, "As in a fairy tale? Ah, you are too *romantique, cherie.* He was the love of my life from the beginning, even when we fought like, what is it, a cat and a dog? But, my dear, one never comes to '*un but heureux'*, a happy ending, and resides there forever. The only thing that *is* forever... is love itself."

She looks up once more, Joie held tightly in her arms, at the portrait of Charles.

"To remain close despite each other's flaws, to love enough to allow one another's differences. To decide all over again each day to let love be what it is—imperfect and profound." Her voice grows so soft it's almost a whisper. "... and still to believe that you belong, always, to one another, no matter what. This is love always. *Toujours. Amour.*"

Le Maintien
Bearing...

Gabrielle invites me to join her for an evening of ballet at Garnier's masterpiece, The Paris Opera. This extravagant building with its Belle Époque interiors was the inspiration and setting for "The Phantom of the Opera."

As we enter the vast marble lobby one can see it was created not only as a showcase for the arts, but for the audience attending them.

Gabrielle leads me up the grand staircase, its winged statues holding their flaming torches, aloft, then through a hall leading into a private box. Tonight we'll see two ballets, Les Préludes, followed by Swan Lake.

I look around the rich interior. "Oh Gabrielle. A box! Really, you shouldn't have."

"*Non*! Don't you dare utter my least favorite American expression," she laughs.

I cease protesting and settle down to enjoy the magnificence of the red and gold auditorium, the huge chandelier that plays a central role in "Phantom," the fanciful ceiling painted by Chagall. Soon enough the curtain rises.

Les Préludes, famed for its dramatic portrayal of the struggle between life and death begins. The corps de ballet clad in flowing grey, white and black costumes dance so passionately, they seem to almost duel with one another. Then suddenly with great majesty, a dancer takes the stage and immediately possesses it. For as long as she is present, she fills the space. And without her, the stage feels emptied.

After applauding through several curtain calls, Gabrielle and I remain in our box for intermission.

"You are enjoying the ballet, Suzanne?"

"*Beaucoup.* The dancers are amazing. And there's one in particular..."

"*Oui.* You mean Cecile, *bien sur.* She is indeed special. She possesses such... *maintien.*"

"*Maintien?*"

"*Oui. Maintien* ,' bearing,' it is a term most often used in the dance."

"Good posture, refinement?"

"*Oui.* But there is more to it than that... I remember Madame Grenier saying that it is 'to wear the head fit for a crown.'"

"You mean 'has' a head fit for a crown?"

"*Non.* I mean 'to wear.' 'To have' means the head one was born with. One had no choice in the matter. *N'est-ce pas?*"

"*C'est vrai.*"

"But to wear means the head one chooses to wear, the self one chooses to be. *Maintien* is the heart's courage to live life well, to meet its challenges and to do so with grace, the shoulders straight and head held high. To dance without fear. *Vous comprenez?*"

"*Oui*, but how does one arrive there I wonder? You can't just decide to 'wear' a head fit for a crown, to be courageous and graceful..."

Gabrielle picks up the evening's program and looks at it. "*Non, cherie*, you cannot just, as you say, decide. One must practice, practice, practice... just as Cecile did."

She hands me the program. The cover features a picture of, 'Cecile Trondeaux, Prima Ballerina.'

"As a patron of the ballet, I came to know her many years ago... I still can see her as a young girl, when she first joined us, how sweet she was, how nervous. Coming to the Paris ballet, she apprenticed under one of the most brilliant and cruel ballet masters who ever lived. Many dancers left the company because of him, victims of his personality. But Cecile stood up to him, determined to learn all he had to teach. *De plus en plus* she chose to wear 'the head fit for the crown,' even when her feet were bloody and she wondered how she could go on. Some afternoons she would come to see me, not to complain, just to be in sympathetic company for a while, before returning to her labors." Gabrielle acknowledges someone waving at her from a nearby box. "And this same *maintein* that made her the prima ballerina she is onstage, has allowed her to endure, and to triumph over, some very hard times in her life away from the stage."

I look at my program again. Cecile in her costume from Swan Lake, yards of white tulle surrounding her, smiles up at the camera. A shining crown is held in place by the soft white wings that curve gracefully around her face.

L'Opera begins to darken, again the curtain rises, this time on Swan Lake. Every dancer before me is exceptional, but as the story progresses, I become impatient for one entrance alone.

At last she arrives on stage. Playing the twin roles of the good Odette and the evil Odile, at one moment Cecile moves with the fluid motion of a swan, at another with the sensuality of a human seductress. Her body conveys every mood and motive, exuding a grace that only appears to be effortless.

She loses herself and all of us along with her, in the story, all the emotions of triumph and heartbreak. And through it all, I see in her body, in her face, in her attitude, majesty of bearing—a way of carrying herself across a stage or through her life.

Too soon the performance comes to an end. The stage grows deep with flowers of every hue. Cecile bows humbly again and again, sharing the applause and her bouquets with the rest of the company.

At last the heavy curtain descends and remains, the lights come up. The audience disperses as Gabrielle and I sit, still watching the stage.

The huge room is almost empty when Gabrielle turns to me. "Oh, Suzanne," she says, eyes shining, "I could tell you as many tales as Scheherazade and never express the word as well as Cecile has just shown it to you. *C'est du maintein.*"

La Sensualité
Sensuality...

On a sunny day Gabrielle and I visit the *Musée Rodin* not so much for the sculptures as the roses that are starting to bloom at this time of year, acres of roses of every shape and color, intoxicating to the eye.

We lunch on the shady side of the *Hotel Biron*, the magnificent mansion in which the *Musée* is housed. The food is excellent but my mind turns to this afternoon's chore. The purchase of new underwear means a boring trip to a department store. But when I ask Gabrielle to recommend one she surprises me by clapping her hands excitedly.

"*Ma chère*, one does not go to *Printemps* or even *Bon Marché* for that kind of thing. Not when one is in Paris! I know a most wonderful woman who sews exquisite lingerie, made to order only. To wear it is to wear the wings of butterflies, so delicate, and the fit—*c'est impeccable!*"

"That sounds lovely, Gabrielle... but it's not something Jon cares about."

"But *cherie*, you don't buy it only for Jon," she looks at me questioningly, "do you?"

I look back at her. "I don't?"

Gabrielle rearranges the linen napkin on her lap then looks across at me. "How to say this Suzanne. One of a woman's most precious gifts is her sensuality, something she explores and enjoys with another, *oui*. But also as her private treasure. To pleasure herself with the touch of fine silk, the taste of a luscious piece of chocolate, the velvety scent of a rose... why would a woman not offer to herself what she would bestow on a lover? Who, after all, should enjoy an exquisite piece of lingerie more, she who wears it or he who sees it?"

I breathe in the heavy scent of roses around us. I know of course that what Gabrielle says is true. And yes, I remember when I was younger feeling much more sensual than I do now, though that sensuality was usually directed at a lover more than to myself, rising and falling with his level of interest. My first husband, a sports fan, had been more interested in the passes a quarterback makes than any made by me. Once, standing in a lingerie department, I'd heard myself say aloud, "Well, no need to shop here unless they sell jockey shorts."

What would have happened I think if I'd bought something gorgeous *just* for me? Would it have saved my marriage? Hardly. But it might have helped save my sanity.

Alright I decide on the spot. I'll try for the first time ever to explore the sensual me *for me* without the benefit of a husband, boyfriend or even a one night-stand. I'll get just one set of that special lingerie. My mind turns to my stash of traveler's checks.

"Well. If you think bras and panties are *that* important I might get a set. What do these things cost anyway?"

A huge smile lights my friend's face. "They're very expensive, *bien sur*. So we will start you off with only two or three sets!"

"Two or three? *Mon Dieu!*"

"Now *cherie*," she admonishes, "you shall just have to trust me about this." She signals the waiter for the check. "Just think of it as the beginning of your *thérapie sensualité.*"

We visit Edmée's shop that same afternoon. I'd never before known the luxury of having something made just for me. Edmée herself helps me select the most flattering color, the perfect weight of fabric. Taking my measurements and making a decision on the cut and style takes a pleasurable hour, while Gabrielle and Joie sit comfortably enjoying a glass or two of champagne in the reception area.

It is almost a month before my lingerie is finished and when at last I am called to return to the shop I find myself rushing there.

"I think you shall be pleased with what we have created for you, Madame," Edmée murmurs as she conducts me toward me the fitting room with its drapes of ivory satin and huge three way mirror.

She loosens the bow atop an ivory colored box, opens it and smoothes back several layers of tissue, then picks up first the bra then panties and places them upon a velvet drape arranged on a small table next to a chair. "Shall I assist you?"

"*Non,* Madame, *merci,*" my shy American side catches up with me. Besides, this experience is something I want to enjoy completely on my own.

When the door has closed behind her, I quickly strip and leave my clothes in a heap on the elegant floor. Then I lift each piece of the pale peach net and satin creation from the drape and look at it, through it, failing to see the tiny invisible stitches that hold such airy confections together. Very carefully I slide each piece on, fearful that such delicate work will fall apart in my hands, but it is much too well made for that.

Nothing ever in my life has felt this delicious on my body. As Gabrielle said, it feels as though butterfly wings are caressing me. Staring into the mirror I know that even Jon would appreciate these works of art. And the work of art that I am as well. The peach gives my skin a tawny glow and suddenly the way I look makes me feel rather sexy, a bit French, a bit of a wild woman. I'd forgotten how that feels. No, more likely I've never experienced it at all—seeing and feeling myself this sensual and womanly without the benefit of a man telling me I am. I decide that a celebration is called for.

I put my sweater and jeans on over my new purchases, pay Edmée an extraordinary amount of money, kiss her goodbye and leave the shop knowing I have just gotten the best bargain in Paris. Outside I see an ash can and toss my ex-underwear into it.

Then I take the time to go all the way to my

favorite outdoor café, the one with the striped awning and spectacular view of Notre Dame upon the Seine.

Dipping into next week's budget, I order a glass of champagne.

And I decide that yes, I'll need to return to Edmée's for another set of lingerie. Or two.

La Gentillesse
Kindness...

After a morning of shopping and errands Gabrielle and I are tired and thirsty. At the next café in our path we take the only table available. An overwhelmed waiter tries his best to keep up with an increasingly impatient crowd. It's a while before he hurries up to our table.

He reaches out to hand us menus, drops them, picks them up, drops them again. Gabrielle leans down to pick them up and says to him in French, her tone soothing, "There are even more people here than usual today."

"*Oui*, Madame. And I know you have been waiting and in the sun, I am so sor. . ."

"Not at all. My friend and I are in no hurry."

"And there are three special dishes today I must just tell you about."

"Ah, no need to bother with that for us. To make things simple for you we shall have two cheese salads and a half carafe of white wine, please." She hands back the menus. "And may I say that with only one of you and so many of us, you are doing a wonderful job." She smiles up at him and he nervously smiles back.

"And," she laughs, "if that red faced man over there roars like a lion at you again, I shall call the zoo to come and take him away." The waiter's shaky smile dissolves into a grin before he rushes away, menus firmly in hand.

I look at Gabrielle. "That was kind of you."

She positions Joie between our chairs, "Maman used to say that kindness, *gentillesse*, is the one bank account which one may spend recklessly and never overdraw... and what a bargain since it costs us nothing."

"Ah, here is our friend again, already." The waiter returns carrying a full rather than the half carafe Gabrielle has ordered. "*Un petite cadeau*" he says, offering it with a proud smile.

"*Merci beaucoup*," Gabrielle responds as he fills our glasses with a happy flourish

Everyone is eventually served, the frenzy of the café dies down and we enjoy a pleasant lunch.

Later in the day Gabrielle and I have parted and I'm walking back toward my flat, when the concierge of my building comes to mind. She's always so friendly to me, stopping whatever she is busy with, as she listens patiently to my faltering attempts to speak French, replying to me slowly and carefully so that I can understand her native tongue.

What a simple kindness it seems to me now to buy her another flowering plant like those she enjoys fussing over in the windows of her flat.

I stop at the small florist shop down the street and choose a bright red begonia from the wire stand outside. When I tell him it's a gift, the shopkeeper chooses a bright red matching bow from the box beside him and adds it to the pot, then asks me to wait a moment before disappearing back inside his store.

It's almost six and I wait a little impatiently, shifting the pot back and forth until he rushes back outside. "When one gives a flower," he says, "one should receive a flower as well." He hands me a single long stemmed white rose done up in cellophane, tied with a soft green ribbon.

"*Merci… merci beaucoup*," I tell him. He grins at me, makes a little bow and wheels the wire stand inside, closing the door and his shop for the night.

I stand on the sidewalk for a moment savoring the sweetness of much more than the scent of this rose. And I remember how kindness is a bank account that is never overdrawn and costs us nothing… how it can yield such huge returns… change someone's day or even their life, completely.

Walking down the street toward my flat I begin to hum, then laugh out loud when I realize the name of the tune… "Pennies From Heaven."

Le Mystère
Mystery...

The times in one's life to confide intimately in another occur far less often than most women imagine. Just as one leaves something to the imagination by wearing a filmy negligee, add something to a conversation by not saying all that is on your mind. Too much detail bores even the dearest of friends and more so a lover.

Prendre Son Temps
Taking one's time...

Allow yourself the time to pause and savor—a glass of wine, a conversation, your child's smile—whatever is before you, in this moment. This is the ancient privilege of princes.

La Souciance, Le Loup
Worry, The Wolf at the Door...

Worry is fear trying to prove why it should exist. There *is* no wolf at the door—nothing terrible is waiting to happen to you. And even if there is a wolf, you cannot prevent its entry into your life nor anticipate its arrival time.

Juillet
July

Se Faire Plaisir
Pleasing Oneself...

We've spent the day finishing the setup of Gabrielle's computer in her flat and in starting to teach her how to use it, something we've been too busy touring Paris to get to. Suddenly she pushes herself back from the keyboard. "I can learn no more today, *cherie*! My brain —*il est fatigué*!" She stands up and stretches, puts her hands on her hips and grins. "Besides, Suzanne, you have worked much too hard. So Joie and I shall take you to *la plage* this afternoon!"

"But... the beach is a day's train ride away from here, even if we take the TGV," I look at her as though she has heatstroke. She just smiles and scoops up Joie, who has started to wag her tail at the word '*plage*.'

"Sure," I say wryly, "let's all go to the beach." We leave the flat and I allow myself to be led across the *Pont Neuf* and down the right bank.

I hear the beach before I see it. A live band on a small platform next to the Seine is going full blast.

Then I'm amazed to see a strip of white sand running along the parapet next to the river. On it are deck chairs, blue and white striped umbrellas, food vendors, children playing. People are diving into a huge inflatable swimming pool.

"*La plage de Paris*," says Gabrielle proudly, "brings the beach to those who cannot go South in the summer."

We descend the steps and claim two chaise lounges on either side of an umbrella. Joie carefully inspects the sand around us.

Gabrielle adjusts her wide brimmed hat, neatly arranges the skirt of her sundress around her, "Your sister will be here soon, *oui*? The children should enjoy this."

"They'll love it! I better email her to bring their swim suits."

I move my legs into the sun, "You know I miss those kids so much, it's been over a year since I've seen them," a sigh escapes me, "but I dread their visit. Mollie insists the three of them stay with me. And you know the size of my flat."

"*Mais*, there are such charming little hotels all over the left bank. And summer rates are quite low this time of year."

"I know. I told Mollie that but she insists that since we haven't seen each other in such a long time..."

"... that the two of you should be, how do you say, are joined at the leg?"

"At the hip."

She giggles, "at the hip, then."

"When Mollie makes up her mind about anything, that's it. That's how it's been all our lives."

"And this has made you happy?"

"It's worked for Mollie. And it's easier for me to let her have her way," I reach for Joie, who quickly evades my grasp. "I know what I'll do, I'll tell her the flat's being painted."

"Why not to just say the truth? That it's too much to have them with you?"

"Mollie's feelings will be hurt."

"Ah then, perhaps it has come the time to hurt them. And for you to stop worrying about it."

"*Excuses-moi?*"

She picks Joie, who protests mightily, up from the sand. "It's Mollie herself who decides if her feelings are hurt. *C'est vrai?* And will you, Suzanne, spend the rest of your life trying always to please everyone else? Besides," I see her make a decision to change tacts, "you would perhaps be doing something nice to find a lovely *chambre* for her, *n'est-ce pas?* "

"Perhaps."

I watch people stroll in the sand along the river. I love my sister. But truth be told, I've resented it all my life as I've given in to her demands. My attempts to give her, as well as everyone else, exactly what they want, are part of that old female problem, the need to please. That's the reason deciding to come to Paris despite Jon's objections was so important to me.

I stand up, "Why don't I get us some lemonade?"

"That would be lovely of you. And *cheri* ?"

"*Oui?*"

"In France we say… 'Please yourself and the world will try to please you as well. Forget yourself and the world forgets you as well,'" she smiles gently, "I don't mean to become the lecturer of you. I only hope you will try to please yourself, put yourself first, more of the time."

"I know." I reach down to pick up my purse, then walk toward the beverage stand.

Waiting in the long line, I recall something another dear friend once said to me—that putting ourselves first is like being on an airplane and putting on your own oxygen mask before helping someone else with theirs. It's what's best for them as well as you. But, really, I think—it's putting on your own mask, even if there's only one mask, even fighting someone else if you must, in order to breathe.

But even thinking this makes my heart beat faster. The concept seems so radical, so cruel, so... Selfish. One of those words it's been ingrained in me to never, ever be accused of. I can't help but wonder if Mollie will decide that selfish is exactly what I'm being.

At last I collect the lemonades and walk back to Gabrielle.

"*Merci beaucoup.*"

"*De rien...* and Gabrielle, you're right about me trying too hard to please other people. In America we call it 'the disease to please,' something a lot of women have in common, although obviously not *all* women, " I smile, "I've got to start getting over it now instead of later."

She puts Joie down, who immediately trots away as far as her leash will allow.

"So. I've decided that there's won't be a painter in my flat when Mollie visits."

"*Non?*"

"Nope. Just me, *moi, toute seule.*" My heart tap dances all over again when it hears my plans out loud.

"Brava, Suzanne!"

"But I'll need your help,"

"Anything, *cherie!*"

I adjust the chaise to allow myself more sun. "Help me find the most wonderful little hotel for Mollie, something a bit luxurious."

Gabrielle adjusts her sunhat, so that all I can see is her smile, "Ah… something that would 'please yourself' if you stayed there?"

"*Exactement!*"

At this moment, I have just begun to learn that putting oneself first does cost something—the safety of saying Yes, and sometimes the displeasure of others.

But I already know that pleasing myself, making my happiness my own responsibility, is its own reward. One I can no longer afford to surrender.

Le Calme
Poise...

Gabrielle and I are browsing through a bookshop on the *Champs-Elysées*, one of the few to carry English as well as French titles.

She's two aisles away, when I notice "LaCroix, The Man and His Vision" in the history section.

The pictures inside include some of Gabrielle. Here she is in evening dress at the opera; standing behind Charles as he speaks at a podium; sitting beside him on a sofa as they smile at each other.

The last picture in the book catches at my heart. Gabrielle stands alone accepting the *Légion d'Honneur*, bestowed on Charles posthumously by the President of France. Impeccably clad in black, her expression is serene.

"Ah. This was the saddest time of my life." She looks over my shoulder, having come to stand beside me in the empty aisle. "Still, I was so proud of Charles on that day. He deserved all the recognition he received," she touches the page gently, "and more."

Still staring at the picture I asked, "How on earth did you get through it, Gabrielle... you seem so at ease, so poised."

"There was no other choice in the matter, Suzanne. Aside from loving him all my life, representing Charles in the way he would prefer, was the one remaining gift

I had to give him... to remind others of the soldier of peace my husband was, by my own demeanor."

"But it couldn't have been easy... to be on public display like that."

"From a very young age, I was taught that one's poise is one's shield...," she takes the book from me and replaces it carefully on the shelf, "a shield of protection that reveals only what one chooses to." A large group of people from a tour bus enters the shop.

The noise builds, a cell phone rings, and I lead the way outside. The *Champs* is Paris' busiest avenue and we briefly join the surge of bodies hurrying forward, before turning into a side street. We are to meet a friend at *Voisin*, one of the smaller restaurants Gabrielle prefers.

'I like the idea of having poise as a shield... as protection." I take Gabrielle's arm as we walk along.

"*Oui*... sometimes in French we call it *l'équilibre*— retaining one's balance. Or *le calme*—to remain quiet."

"Or, we might call it *la tranquillité*... peace of mind." She tosses back her silky scarf of green blowing forward in the breeze. "But all it really is... is the outer evidence of the unshakeable inner."

I listen to her heels click along the sidewalk beside me. "I could use some of that "unshakeable inner' right now in my life."

A sedan stops at a distant corner and a fulsome redhead, clad in couture from head to toe, emerges and rushes up the sidewalk toward us.

Gabrielle pauses in front of the restaurant and turns to me. "But it is always there for you, in you, whenever you need it, Suzanne, a protection you may assume at will. After all, it is part of your legacy... the French may have more words for it, but it was an American woman, Jacqueline, who showed the world what true poise looks like."

"Ah, Nina," she calls out, "*te voila, mon amie*.!"

Kisses of greeting are exchanged all around but I go through the motions automatically, images of Jacqueline Kennedy running through my mind. Not just the stoic face behind the black veil, but her presence—elegant and warm, poised and private—as she created her own style and her own rules, in her own life... unshakeable to the end.

Nina stands back and gives us both a long look. "And what, my two dears, were you in such deep conversation about?"

"Ah," replies Gabrielle, "we were speaking of something that we all must have in our wardrobe."

"Something simple and timeless to wear?"

"*Bien sur!*"

"A little black dress? A suit from Chanel?"

The *maitre'd* opens the door to welcome us inside.

"More basic than that, Nina," Gabrielle smiles at me, "and it never goes out of style."

La Magie
Magic...

Gabrielle, Joie's tail tick-tocking beneath her arm, leads me down a small left bank side street to *Lé Samovar d'Argent*, The Silver Samovar, a tiny café tucked neatly between a boulangerie and a cobbler. Its two windows, draped in emerald green cloth, are tall and thin.

The door opens into a charming room, tables covered in more emerald cloth, a small lamp aglow on each. The exotic scent hanging in the air might be cinnabar.

A beaded curtain on the opposite wall parts to reveal an older, heavy-set woman, still attractive despite a wealth of rouge and jewels. Her silvery hair is pulled back into a tight chignon; her long black dress is like a robe.

"*Ah, ma très chère Madame LaCroix*" she opens her arms and she and Gabrielle kiss on each cheek.

"*Enchantée de vous revoir, Madame Tatiana.* This is my dear friend Suzanne from America who I have brought to see you."

Madame Tatiana switches to English. "Ah, but how wonderful. Welcome Suzanne. Come. Sit here at this most favorite table," she gestures toward a particularly cozy spot. When we are seated, she proffers a huge velvet pillow for Joie, who regards it with a regal air before accepting it.

Halfway through the beaded curtain she turns back toward us, "Ah Madame LaCroix, I have those cakes that you so favor, ordered especially for you."

"*Merci*, Madame. *Cherie*, you will adore these sweets. They are made by a Russian baker, a friend of Madame's."

"You called her to say we were coming?'

"*Non*. But she always seems to know when I will visit."

"Then perhaps what I've heard about Madame Tatiana's abilities are true? That she can tell the future, and that she casts spells?"

Gabrielle laughs. "*Oui*, she reads the tea leaves. And as to the casting of spells, this is the art of any woman, *n'est-ce pas*? "

"That may apply more to French women than Americans."

Soon Madame reappears followed by a waiter much smaller than the tray he staggers beneath. On it sits a silver samovar at least two feet high, glinting with scroll work and mother of pearl. A second elfin waiter bears a tray laden with cups, saucers and other accoutrements. Madame herself carries a cut glass plate of the special cakes which she places ceremoniously on our table.

"Madame, you are too kind. Will you honor us by pouring and sharing our tea?" asks Gabrielle.

Madame seems delighted to accept the invitation

and carefully settles herself behind the samovar. After the proper amount of time for steeping, she reaches forward daintily to draw the tea from the silver spigot. She and Gabrielle chat in English, French and Russian about various friends. I half-listen happily while devouring one sweet cake after another, until I realize Gabrielle is speaking to me. "Suzanne, ask Madam about what it is you want to know."

I swallow one more sugary bite, "Well Madame… I was wondering if you can read a person's future in the tea leaves? And," I'm more than a little embarrassed, "if it's true what I heard, that you know how to cast spells."

Madame's laugh is as deep as Joie's velvet pillow. "*Oui*, I read the leaves. But the truth?" she lowers her voice though the room is empty; "I read what is in a person's eyes, more than in their leaves. You for instance, Suzanne, your fears and your hopes have to do with… love, do they not? *Non*, do not answer, I say only what I see. However," she smiles at Gabrielle, "when it comes to spells, Madame LaCroix could teach you as well as I could." She smiles and pats Gabrielle's hand as the door opens to five people, a sizeable crowd for the room. She rises quickly to greet them, "so perhaps she will be so kind?"

Surprised, I turn toward Gabrielle who breaks off a bit of a cake, nibbles it, then turns her gaze on me. "I think Tatiana is too modest about her abilities and much too generous about mine. But tell me Suzanne, what is this fascination with spells you have?"

"Well, it's not that I want to make Jon do anything against his will. But sometimes I think how wonderful it would be to cast a spell, *un ensorcellement sensual* over him, so that, perhaps when I return to New York things might be more like, you know, when we first fell in love all those years ago. We were so crazy about each other back then."

I look at the leaves in my teacup and then at Gabrielle, "Was Madame Tatiana just teasing me? Or do you really know some sort of...?"

"I know nothing of what's done with top hats and rabbits but," she smiles, touches her head and breast, "but a small something of *la magie*, that of the head and the heart."

Joie stirs on her pillow and yawns with a little squeak that makes us laugh.

"However it works..."

Gabrielle takes a sip of tea. "*Donc, ma cherie*, it seems that what you want is a spell to return Jon to a sweeter, happier time of your love. *Oui?*"

"That's it!" I sit on the edge of the overstuffed chair.

"The spell I shall teach you then," she pronounces in a mock serious tone, "Is called A Journey into the Past."

I lean further forward, "Time travel?"

She laughs softly, "Something like that."

Near us, the curtain beads rattle and part as

Tatiana's waiters enter the room carrying a samovar and its' accompaniments to the other table.

Gabrielle puts down her teacup and leans close to me. "Tell me Suzanne, when you first came to know Jon, what was he like as a man? What was it that drew you to him?" Her voice is low and soothing, "Close your eyes and relax, think back to that time… when you had just met him."

I lie back in the soft cushions; eyes closed and breathe in… is it sandalwood? I begin to drift back through the years to when I first met Jon. My friend Ed had badgered me about meeting Jon for so long that I finally gave in. I was tired after work and just wanted to get the evening over with… but then I walked through the door of Bennie's in the Village and there he was, those great dark eyes, that smile, and somehow the night became an enchanted one. I remember our long conversation. Jon was an adventurer and his stories of traveling all over the world were fascinating. And he, amazingly, seemed fascinated by me as well, wanting to hear all about me and my life. So clearly I see him, sitting there… cherished memories follow one another… the first time he kissed me, suddenly, deeply, before turning to walk out the door… my excitement when I dressed for our evenings together… our feverish passion for each other. . . how much, how very much I wanted him, his body and his heart.

Gabrielle's soft voice enters my reverie. "I see you

remembering, feeling him from that time, *Cherie. C'est merveilleux, n'est-ce pas?*"

"Yes," I answer dreamily, "he was… we were… marvelous."

"And do you want to have the Jon, and the you of that time, come to life again?"

"More than anything," I sigh.

A crash from the Café's back room and shouts in Russian and French jerk me back to reality.

I sit up in my chair. "Tatiana was right… you *do* know how to cast a spell, Gabrielle." I sigh, "but already it's disappearing into thin air."

"But it wasn't I who cast it."

"Who then?"

"Why," she smiles at me, "it was you, *bien sur!*"

"But you told me… you said…"

"I ask some questions, Suzanne… the memories of your own heart made the past into the present again, turned Jon into who he once was. Again."

She cocks her head to one side. "Shall I tell you the true secret *de la magie*, Cherie?"

"*Oui.*"

"That you yourself are the caster of spells, the magician who, with the power of your heart calls forth love *or* casts it aside—and you do it with but a memory, a word, a look. If you do not prefer the Jon of the present, cast a spell by seeing him, by loving him, as you did in the past. And bewitch yourself as well Suzanne, because you also are different, you also have changed since those times."

Madame Tatiana drifts back to our table and begins to chat with Gabrielle, their voices as low and melodic as incantations.

I sit silently not really listening to them. Might Gabrielle be right? Have I changed as much, perhaps even more than Jon?

And what if the way back to a happier time in my life *is* by allowing my heart to turn back toward what *was* true between us… until it becomes true again?

The steam from the samovar rises like a spirit through the emerald light of the drapes. Joie dreams curled up on her pillow.

I lie back in the chair again and close my eyes again… inhale the air heavy with sandalwood and cinnabar. Time seems to stretch out and lengthen with this long summer afternoon… as my thoughts reach out across the ocean to Jon, touching him, wanting him, casting a spell that he can never escape… then turning the spell on myself, the passionate loving self I long to recapture and never lose again.

Forgiveness

Pardonner...

On a late June morning Gabrielle and I walk through *Père La Chaise*, Paris' most famous cemetery. Named for Louis XIV's confessor, it's enormous, lush and green. The imaginative architecture of the graves and all the famous people resting here make it a tourist attraction. They come to leave lipstick prints on Oscar Wilde's monument, bourbon and cigarettes at Jim Morrison's.

Up a hill toward the back of the cemetery on a quieter, less busy path are the graves of Gertrude Stein and her long-time companion, Alice B. Toklas. Stein's courage in using language in a new and original way influenced so many important authors and artists and she has long been my personal inspiration and literary Godmother.

We stand before the two small headstones and I reach down to place a nosegay of violets on each one, then the tears I've been holding back have their way.

"Gabrielle, I don't know what I was thinking of coming here this morning. This is probably the worst day of my life," I stare blindly toward her, then she is beside me steadying me. Gently she turns me around, walks me away from the path.

She settles me on an old wooden bench, puts her

arm around me and says nothing for a moment or two, then almost whispers, "Suzanne, *ma chère*, what is it? Has something happened to Jon?"

I find my handbag and fumble in it for a handkerchief. At least I was smart enough not to wear mascara today. "*Oui*, yes, I guess you could say something happened to Jon. Last night or yesterday or whenever it was in New York, he was at a party and ran into an old girlfriend, someone he used to date in college. And they started talking which led to dinner which led to a few bottles of wine which led to the two of them in bed," I stop to wipe my eyes. "He says he knew right away he'd made a big mistake, walked out and came home, then called me. To confess I guess and swear that it will never happen again. But Gabrielle, it doesn't matter whether it ever happens again because as far as I'm concerned," my emotions turn to steel, "our marriage is over. How in the world could I ever, ever trust him after this?"

Gabrielle looks as stricken as I feel.

"Ah, *cherie*, I am so sorry, so sorry for you."

She reaches out to smooth a strand of hair back from my face, "Ah, but this is terrible, terrible for you. And too for poor Jon."

"Obviously not so bad for Jon, since he's the one sleeping around!," Gabrielle's other arm goes around me in a huge soft hug and I let myself lean into her and have a good cry. We stay this way until my tears exhaust themselves and all is quiet again.

I release myself from her arms, sit back and breathe a ragged sigh, "I will never forgive him for what he did to me. Never."

Softly she asks, "Never? You will let your marriage end because there is no forgiveness for him in your heart at all, Suzanne? Even if he may be broken in his own heart as well?"

I feel myself stiffen with surprise, "Are you defending him, Gabrielle?"

"Perhaps I am *ma chère*. Perhaps… someone needs to."

"Well, this is a surprise. You of all people, who had such a devoted marriage," my anger toward Jon turns easily to her.

"That's true. I was devoted to Charles." She reaches out to give my hand a gentle squeeze almost shyly. "He was the love of my life. You know that yes, *cherie*?"

"Yes, I know," I answer impatiently.

"He was my heart, Suzanne, my very heart." She clasps her hands in her lap, looks down at them. "And yet," very slowly she lifts her gaze to meet mine, "and yet. I did to him, what Jon has done to you."

She sees the effect her words have on me. "I shock you," she looks straight ahead.

"I don't understand."

"But Jon needs you to understand it," her face is pale, determined, "It is for *both* your sakes I speak of something very difficult for me."

"Gabrielle, what exactly happened?"

For the first time ever I see her falter, "Please understand, *cherie*, that things happen with the people in our lives, for which they must carry the blame..."

"I should think so."

"But then, for our sake and theirs, if we love them, we try to understand and then... then to forgive them."

"Gabrielle, I know that Jon..."

"Suzanne, you know *nothing*," a sudden flash of anger, "You may think you know him, you may have lived with him many years, but you cannot know all of what is in his heart," she brushes away what may have been a tear, "as Charles did not know all of what was in mine. So. Will you hear what I have to say or do you chose to not?"

"Yes. Alright."

She sits very still and looks out over the cemetery. "When Charles and I met we fell in love and married quite rapidly," her hands knot together in her lap, "I knew that as a devoted and *oui*, an ambitious diplomat, his office demanded much of his time, much of his life and I accepted this. All that mattered was that we were together and that we were," she smiles sadly, "we were so happy."

A man and woman approach, consult a map and pause at the Stein and Toklas graves. Gabrielle is silent until they make their way down the path.

"The third year of our marriage, Charles was made

Ambassador to Morocco, a most grand promotion and of course, a challenging one. We moved to Rabat and he was busy from the moment we arrived. Often he was traveling about the country to places it would not be so easy for a woman to go and so he must go alone," She removes a handkerchief from her handbag. "I was so proud of Charles, so happy for him. But as the months passed he travelled more and more. And alone in a strange country, I became lonely." A sparrow lands near us and busily pecks along the ground.

"It happened that in time I came to know a group of other French who were living there, artists and writers, who became my friends. I was no longer so alone," her voice trembles. "There was… one friend, a painter, wonderful at capturing the people's colorful dress, the exotic kasbahs. Always I had wanted to paint but never was brave enough to try. This friend, he saw my longing. And he *made* me to paint, brought paints and canvas to my home, began to teach me. He opened up this new world for me and as I began to paint, I spent much of my days with him, our easels side by side in some beautiful place. While painting we spoke of our lives, became close friends but then… this closeness of our minds deepened into," Gabrielle watches as the sparrow flutters away, "a closeness that was more than friendship."

With enormous self control she continues, "Suzanne, I do not justify my behavior, from the first moment I knew it was wrong what we did... always these moments of passion were followed by such regret," a tear is quickly touched away, "and so I ended the affaire."

"And did Charles ever find out?"

"Of course," she turns to look at me. "Like Jon I too, had to tell my beloved... and pray that he would somehow find it in his heart to forgive me."

"And he forgave you," I think of Charles' portrait on the wall.

"All he said was," Gabrielle's voice breaks, "'You must have been so lonely to do this. Please forgive *me* for making you this lonely.'"

Now my own tears return and I reach out to hug her. For only a moment she rests lightly on my shoulder before slowly sitting back, composing herself.

"My dear, dear Suzanne. I beg of you to try, even though I know your heart is broken, to try to understand that we can never know why another person makes some terrible mistake. But if somehow we can bestow '*pardonner*', forgiveness, love still has a chance, we still have a chance. All is not lost."

I lean back against the bench. My gaze falls on the headstones of Gertrude and Alice, lying peacefully side by side after a long and devoted life together, one that surely must have required much forgiveness from each of them toward the other.

I'm suddenly exhausted by a cascade of feelings,

hurt, confusion, anger. But at the very bottom of my heart, along with what I know is love after all for Jon, there now lies the tiniest ray of hope. If Gabrielle could love Charles so passionately and do what she did, perhaps Jon really does love me as he kept pleading with me to believe during that terrible phone call.

I hear a long sigh and realize it's mine. "Gabrielle, I don't know what will happen to Jon and me. But thank you for sharing with me all you have. I can only imagine how hard it was." I fold my damp handkerchief away, snap my handbag shut "but perhaps you're right... maybe, maybe if you and Charles survived... perhaps we do have a chance... more of one than I was going to allow us anyway."

"And," I look at her face, older now than I've ever seen it, "I hope you can forgive me, for my rudeness and impatience with you. I had no idea..."

Gabrielle smiles and touches my shoulder. She slips her own handkerchief into her bag and gives a little shrug. "Oh, Suzanne, there is not a thing to forgive you for," she stands, straightens the jacket of her suit, then turns and reaches her hand out for mine.

She looks at the violets on the graves across the path. "Come along now, *ma chère*. I shall take you to a little café that I know of and we shall start with a strong *aperitif* before our lunch. *Oui?*

"*Oui, ma chère*," I answer.

Solitude
Solitude...

It's early July and Gabrielle and I are spending the day in the *Bois de Boulogne*, a huge park that includes gardens, lakes, horse racing tracks, even a small chateau; all connected by winding paths.

We walk along one of these paths Joie trotting beside us, toward the greenhouses.

"This is one of my favorite places to spend time alone," says Gabrielle, "there is so much to see and explore here."

"You like being along here?"

"*Oui*, as much as I adore the company of friends like yourself, *cherie*, I enjoy time to myself."

"I don't so much enjoy time alone as tolerate it. I was hoping I'd feel differently here in Paris with so much to do and see but," we walk past a couple holding hands, "It just feels like the world is made for two. Even Noah put the animals in his boat *à deux*."

"*C'est vrai*, he did, but only for the purpose of pro-creation," she laughs. She picks up Joie. "Enjoying one's solitude is often an acquired taste."

We enter a long arbor thick with climbing roses, a shadowy, perfumed corridor that we walk slowly through.

"How very lonely I felt when I first came to Paris, knowing no one, far from my family and my beloved

Maman for the first time. Then I met Charles and I was no longer alone. Until his career kept us moving always to the next post. Then, as you know," she touches my arm, "it became something I had to learn. And in time I was grateful for the pleasure in solitude I came to know."

She hugs Joie to her. "I wish I could give that gift to you *cherie*, such a precious one it is, to enjoy one's self with oneself. Especially since I shall be leaving next week you know, to spend the rest of the summer on the *Côte d'Azur.*"

Gabrielle has mentioned joining friends on the coast a couple of times, but somehow I've thought it would be after I'd returned to New York. And I've seen her so often since my arrival, I haven't been on my own that much.

Back in New York, part of the idea of coming here to live in Paris had been to be alone, to see if I'd gotten any better at it than I had been in the past. Obviously I haven't.

We exit the arbor and stand for a moment in the sunlight of the courtyard by the greenhouses. Gabrielle lets Joie off the leash and she scampers away quickly. We sit on one of several benches scattered about.

I say almost timidly, "So. Since I will be by myself in Paris for the next few weeks, I might as well try to start liking it better now. What are the things you enjoy most about it?"

She thinks a while before speaking.

"Well, *ma chère*.... one reason I enjoy it is quite simple—the freedom to do as one pleases, when one pleases. How often I leave my flat to do one thing, change my mind and go in the opposite direction, or dine on cake for lunch and skip dinner, or spend an entire day in my dressing gown with a fascinating novel. One can do these things in the company of another, *oui*, but not so easily." She claps her hands at Joie, who is giving a boxer several times her size a hard time.

"Then there is the pursuit of one's own interests, intellectual, creative or otherwise, such as the play you're working on. Writing is a solitary practice, so I understand." A man and woman with a picnic basket walk arm in arm past us to sit on the next bench.

"There are so many pleasures that it's assumed are only to be shared," her eyes brighten. "What fun to discover this is not so! *Par exemple*, women will not often dine alone, especially in one of the finer restaurants. But if a woman enjoys great food and wine, this is the perfect way to fully appreciate them," she chuckles delightedly, "and you will never get better service in your life."

Joie and the boxer chase each other back and forth across the lawn as the picnicking couple watch. "And one can do this with so many other things, attend an opera or a play, or just walk along the Seine, experiencing it all in a completely different and fascinating way when the only companion is the self."

"But," Gabrielle, chin in hand, gazes out past the

lawns, "the most important thing of all is that… there is a grace in being by oneself, a comfort in the quiet of it. Solitude provides a chance to contemplate our lives. It gives us a deeper understanding of our true thoughts, and emotions, our dreams. If we are never alone, how can we possibly know what we truly want? How can we know who we are?"

A summer breeze seizes a bright blue kite and waltzes it across the sky above us. We watch until it is out of sight.

"There's more to it than I can think of now Suzanne, things you can only find out for yourself, by yourself. But I promise you that the rewards are many. I was reminded of this again," her eyes smile into mine, "when Charles died."

We sit in silence, until we're distracted by the shouts from the next bench. Rex, the boxer, is ignoring the calls of his frustrated master in his fascination with Joie.

"*Joie, retournes-ici tout de suite,*" Gabrielle calls out. Joie trots over meekly, followed by Rex.

"Rex," she says, as we dissolve in laughter, "*retournes a ton maitre, s'il te plait.*"

At last we gather Joie up and walk toward an enormous greenhouse while Rex watches us mournfully, leashed at his owners' side.

Once we're inside, Gabrielle turns to me. "I hope that was helpful, Suzanne."

"It was," I nod, "but there's a lot to learn."

"And I'll have to be alone, to learn it," I say, wishing the lesson could be delayed for just a while longer, by the pleasure of her company.

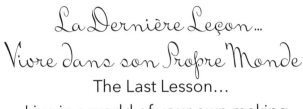

La Dernière Leçon...
Vivre dans son Propre Monde
The Last Lesson...
Live in a world of your own making

The last time I see Gabrielle or rather as she prefers to say, "the last time until the next" is at the *Gare de Lyon*. She is to leave Paris for her summer holiday and has asked me to lunch at *Le Train Bleu* before she boards the TGV to the South.

Le Train Bleu is as classic as Gabrielle herself, an exquisite restaurant from the early 1900's, named after the legendary *Train Bleu*, France's version of the Orient Express. Its walls and ceilings are covered with beautiful murals, its appointments plainly from a time in which travelers knew that the journey was as important as the destination.

We toast each other with *Kir Royales* but today I look at more of my lunch than I eat. I'm going to miss my dear friend and mentor a great deal. I wonder how much I have really understood and absorbed of all she has tried to teach me. And I wonder if we will ever meet again.

As attentive a companion as ever, Gabrielle smiles softly and reaches across the table to take my hand in hers.

"I shall miss you, *ma chère* Suzanne. "

"And I you, Gabrielle. Terribly. I have loved our time together."

"Then we shall probably have more of the same."

"I hope so. *Merci mille fois.* For all you've taught me. Paris won't be the same without you."

"Ah. You are kind to say that. But it will be. Paris is always the same. And she has much more to reveal to you than I could in a hundred lifetimes. Paris is a world of her own making... just as you live in the world which you make."

"I live in the world, but I don't know that I create it. And I certainly can't control all that's going on."

"*Mais non*! And how boring it would be if you could. But I do not mean the world outside *cherie*, but the one within, where you alone are absolute ruler.

Inside we make a world of our own; with our kindnesses, with elegance in thought as well as deed," a waiter silently appears and whisks away our plates, "with all the things that truly matter to us; the light on the Seine; the light in your eyes when you speak of Jon. And with the precious friends we allow to become a part of us, as we are of them. As you and I will always be a part of each other. These are the world that we make."

I take Gabrielle's other hand and hold it in mine. We sit this way for what must only be a few seconds but feels much longer. Once again I'm touched not only by her words but by the spirit behind them. I feel a tear come to my eye and brush it away so quickly that she has not seen it.

I stand, "Let me walk you to your train, *ma chère* Gabrielle," I smile at her, "*s'il te plait.*"

Suzanne...

Suzanne...

It's April again and I've almost finished painting the Eiffel Tower.

I'm standing on a ladder for this, since it's the tallest piece of our rather simple stage set.

Here at the M Street Theatre in Brooklyn just about anyone who's willing to paint scenery, and do all the other labor an amateur theatre requires, can get their play put on, as mine will be starting this Friday.

Well, actually I'm being a bit modest. "French Lessons" beat out a dozen other plays for one of this season's slots at M Street. I remain in a state of happy amazement at this.

My trip to Paris took place two years ago. In some ways it feels as though I returned just yesterday, in others as though it's been a decade since Gabrielle instructed me in everything from buying lingerie to the art of solitude.

When I returned to New York that August, I wasn't sure what would be waiting. But it was me, once again in the midst of my life, right where I'd left it.

Since then there have been plenty of changes. Some of my old life and much of my old self is missing, as though I've been smoothed and streamlined into a newer version. I like this me. And I trust her more than I ever have before.

I'm making less money now and I'm still writing

marketing materials, but it's for a group of lobbyists who support the environment, something I believe in. I buy less outer wear than I used to, in order to support my lingerie habit. My relationship with Mollie has changed a lot but it's more real than it was before. I now have a small dog, a mixed breed from the pound, Sophie, who curls around my feet, and keeps me company when I'm writing, which is almost every day.

I miss Gabrielle despite receiving the occasional letter on elegant Hermes paper, or hearing her voice when I pick up the phone and call. I miss Joie, who I understand has the beginnings of silvery fur here and there. Actually, I think about going back to Paris all the time.

And sooner or later, I will.

But for now on this early Spring evening, all I'm thinking of as I reach up, is putting the finishing touches of green paint on the tip of the Eiffel.

Suddenly I hear footsteps hurrying through the lobby. They continue down the aisle in my direction. Looking out I can't see a thing in the darkness, the only light the one on stage, shining down in a halo around me.

A man comes swiftly into its circle. It's my husband.

"Jon! What are you doing here?"

"I thought I'd take my favorite playwright out to dinner, *bien sur*."

I give the top of the Eiffel one more dab of green, then descend the ladder into his waiting arms.

"I married an American, but now it seems I've fallen in love with this French girl," he says.

"Lucky you," I say and kiss him the requisite three times.

Whether or not you have your own wise,
wonderful and charming woman who
teaches you about life, here are a few ideas
and words of encouragement for...

Your Own French Lessons!

Living Well…
avec l'Élégance

- *What is one thing you could do today to add a touch of elegance to your home or office?* Buy a small bouquet for your desk or frame a card from a child as a keepsake? Or simply straightening your desk before you leave your office at day's end?

- *What change in your own manner,* perhaps your style of communicating or the way in which you carry yourself, might make you act and feel more elegant? What personal refinement would give *you* pleasure? How might this change affect your life?

- *What is an activity which to you, has a sense of elegance or grace about it?* Something you don't usually make time for but which gives your life more meaning when you *do*? Possibilities: visiting a museum, arranging flowers, listening to music that touches or inspires you, reading poetry, taking a walk through your neighborhood in the quiet of evening. Make the time for it and notice how it enlarges your life.

Living Well...

avec Joie de Vivre

- *Allow yourself to be more spontaneous.* Embrace life as it occurs, suddenly and magically. For instance, you encounter an old friend as the two of you are rushing in opposite directions down a sidewalk. Stop if only for ten minutes, have a coffee and a real chat with each other.

- *Give yourself a wonderful present—an entire day with absolutely no plans in it,* not a chore, not even a pleasurable plan to see friends. Follow your whims and enjoy whatever direction they take you in. Follow your appetite and indulge yourself without guilt.

- *Deep laughter between good friends or perfect strangers—is not only one of life's greatest pleasures—but one of its healthiest habits.* Give in to what amuses you.

- *Appreciate the moment for its self alone.* Put your work papers down and play with that child who will be an adult before you know it. Tell your loved one that he or she IS the love of your life—and let your actions show it. Stop always going forward and revel in the "Bliss of THIS"... This moment, person, day!

Living Well...
avec Le Cachet

- *Have a sense of your own best style.* Don't confuse what you may like looking *at* on someone else, with what you look your best *in*! If you're not a six foot tall model, frills may not be as flattering as tailored fashions that add sleekness to your silhouette.

- *If you don't have a sense of what looks best on you,* ask for the assistance of a well-dressed friend—or a professional, such as a personal shopper/stylist.

- *Pay attention to the colors you wear.* As you are aware of the cut of clothing looks best on you, know the colors that flatter you and dismiss those that don't.

- *Know the limitations of and dress, your age.* If you are over 40, unless you *live* in the gym, save the short shorts for home. This doesn't mean wearing boring, shapeless outfits for the rest of your life, just presenting you at your best, whatever shape or age you are.

- *Be impeccable!* From your head (even if you get your hair cut at beauty school) to your toes (even if you do your own pedicure) *be perfectly groomed.* Whatever your budget, do it yourself if you must, but be ready to meet the world at your best!

- *Posture!* You've heard this all your life because it's true. Keeping your spine straight is not only wonderful for you physically, it's the most flattering and immediate thing you can do for your figure.

Living Well...
avec L'Ordre

- *The key to order is simplicity, simplicity, simplicity!*

- *Clutter is the enemy of order.* Consign or donate anything you seldom wear or use. You can open any closet, kitchen or dresser drawer, bathroom cabinet and often find things you no longer/seldom use. And it's a kindness to donate things you've no purpose for to someone else who would really appreciate them.

- *Just Desserts!* The more challenging the room (Your office!!! *Mon Dieu!*) the greater the reward! For particularly intimidating rooms or those scary walk in closets reward yourself for getting it done with a treat—dinner at that new (French of course) restaurant you've been coveting, a trip to the movies, or now that there's room in your closet—a new ensemble!

- *Start picking up after yourself!* At the end of the day, as you leave each room, put it in order—gather up the magazines, clear the kitchen counter, straighten your desk. It's lovely the next morning to waken *into* order!

- *Ah, the wisdom of Baby Steps.* If the very thought of any of the above makes your heart race, not with delight, stop and baby step the task at hand. You can accomplish *anything* if you break it into small enough bites. It's wiser to take longer to do something than to be stopped in your stilettos because the steps are too high.

Living Well…
avec L'empathie

- *Empathy arrives the moment we put ourselves in another's place.* This practice alone can bring great peace and understanding to our own lives and the world we all must share.

- *Assume the best of others instead of the worst.*

- *Make a special effort to be empathetic to those you are closest to*—spouse, friends, family. Sometimes we extend more empathy to acquaintances and strangers than to the most important people in our lives.

- *The opposite of empathy is judgment.* Avoid it toward others as you would have them avoid it toward you.

Living Well...

avec l'Amour-Propre

- *At the party of life, what are the special gifts you bring with you*—those characteristics that others remark upon appreciating you for? What is unique about you?

- *Name the ten accomplishments in your life that you are proudest of*—something you created, did or were/are.

- *Name what is most beautiful about you.* Is it the sound of your voice, the shape of your hands, your quick wit and ability to make others laugh?

- *Appreciate your body, As It Is Now...* your breasts, hips, hands, feet, waist—all serve you so faithfully, even when they are tired. Thank your body and care for it –not only with exercise and healthy food, but with pedicures, massages and other "necessary luxuries."

- *If you had one trait of your own to bestow as a gift on a newborn, what would it be?* What would would add happiness or meaning to their life, as it has yours?

- *Is there something you don't appreciate about your-self—a character trait or habit that you would be happier without?* If so, create a strategy to support changing it. Be compassionate and patient with yourself as you change, especially if it's a long time part of your personality.

Living Well...

avec Le Charme et Le Charisme

- *Who is the most charming person you know? What is it that makes her or him so?* Is there a trait of theirs, that would feel authentic and natural to you, should you chose to adopt it? For instance, you notice that a friend is outgoing and puts others at their ease, might you make the effort to do the same?

- *Who is the most charismatic person you know? Why?*

- *What is most charming about you?* What do friends enjoy about you?

- *If you were sending yourself to Charm School what are the new traits or habits you would choose to master?* Would you opt for better manners, improved listening skills, added social and personal confidence? How would you have changed by the time you "graduated?"

Living Well...

avec Les Vacances de Douze Heures

- *If you must, start small, make an hour at a time for yourself* taken from a busy weekend with the children, or *half an hour for a walk and a breath of fresh air* during a long business day. Make this a regular part of your schedule.

- *Take the 12 hour vacation as stated* . Notice how relaxed you feel on your "return." Take it at least once a month, more often when your life is particularly stressed or busy.

- *Notice how the space and time you make for yourself benefits others.* After taking even a small break for yourself, you'll be more patient and pleasant with those who you sometimes resent for "never giving me a moment."

Living Life…
avec La Curiosité

- *At the next event you attend introduce yourself to at least three strangers.* Find out three things about each.

- *At a social event, don't gravitate to and remain with friends without meeting new people.* As well as increasing your circle of friends, you may do a kindness to a stranger who is alone and marooned in her own shyness.

- *Make a professional/networking event personal.* Find out something about people regarding their family, background etc., instead of staying on business. Listen sincerely to the other person, instead of simply waiting your turn to talk about you.

- *At any event, introduce people to one another.* Being a catalyst for others to meet is not only helpful to them but the perfect antidote to one's own shyness.

- *Regarding other people as fascinating (and yet unopened) books is one of the great pleasures of life. Be curious and be enriched by their stories and their lives.*

Living Well…
avec La Paresse

- *When you notice yourself restlessly moving your body,* tapping your feet, your fingers etc, give yourself "permission to rest." How do you feel when you do so?

- *Give your body and your stress levels a break throughout the day.* Start with a good stretch, then relax and either sit or lie down for as little as five minutes. Take a series of good deep breathes and allow yourself to just "do nothing." Notice the effect this has on your body. Take this stillness with you as you enter again into your busy day. Notice its effect.

- *Who do you know who is particularly still or relaxed?* What is the effect on you and others?

Living Well

avec... la Créativité

- *"Audition" possible creative outlets.* Give different activities—writing, painting, pottery, bead-work, *anything*—"a try" to see *if* they are something that is a source of pleasure. You may find more than one creative pursuit that appeals to you.

- *If you've no idea what you'd like to pursue, make an adventure of it!* Take yourself exploring to see what strikes your fancy—visit a bookstore to see what sections and subjects intrigue you, explore a hobby or crafts store. Surf the web and see what direction the waves lead you in.

- *Rejoice in being an amateur, in being unpracticed at whatever you do since perfectionism will stop you in your tracks.* As a child finger paints just for the fun of it, give yourself the gift of pleasure in the moment. And don't compare yourself with others.

- *Make creative appointments for yourself.* Schedule the time and honor it as you would any other.

Living Well

avec... l'Amour Toujours

- *What are the traits and characteristics of your significant other that you most enjoy?* Let him know that you do.

- *How would your relationship change* if you stopped trying to change each other?

- *When having an emotional or heated discussion—*

  - *Let one another speak* his/her mind without interruption. Think about what has been said *before* responding.

  - *Instead of "blaming language" use the formula—"When you... I feel."* For instance "When you don't pay the bills, I feel as though I can't rely on you" instead of "You never remember to pay the bills!"

  - *Do not raise your voice to one another.* For most people this signifies attack.

  - *Slow your pace in speaking.* This helps avoid escalating emotions.

  - *Do not resort to name calling.* Think better of yourself as well as your partner.

- *If emotions are at a high for either one of you—
  wait!* Take a break—a day or at least an hour—
  until you can speak with more clarity and less
  emotional charge.

- *Decide in advance, what you want the outcome of
  your conversation to be.*

• Make every possible confrontation into an
opportunity for partnership.

Living Well
avec... Le Maintien

- *Three important aspects of maintein* are –

  - *Gracefulness*, the *manner* in which we do things—how we move, speak, listen, live.

  - *Graciousness*, our thoughtfulness and generosity toward others.

  - *Equanimity*, the ability to remain calm and collected in any situation.

- *Begin to embody the trait of maintein.* Let the word, the quality itself, become your credo—and guide. Notice the difference between approaching whatever is at hand with *maintein*—or without it.

- *To further inspire yourself, think of someone who for you, is an example of maintein—let her become your model and inner mentor.*

- *While maintein is most certainly a quality of inner bearing, it is an outer one as well.* Good posture, the manner in which one physically carries oneself, taking care of one's body and health through proper diet and exercise all contribute to its expression.

Living Well

avec... La Sensualité

- *When you think of giving yourself pleasure, what is the first thought that comes to mind? Follow it!*

- *Become a connoisseur* of wine, roses or anything else that gives you sensual pleasure. Enjoy learning all about it and explore its different nuances and forms.

- *Buy lingerie that makes you feel absolutely gorgeous. Wear it when you are alone... and not.*

- *Appreciate your own body and its sensuality, without judgment.*

- *Do not save your most beautiful clothes or anything else for a special occasion.* Enjoy them, and the way they make you feel today!

- *Try different ethnic cuisines, especially those that are new to you.* Learn to cook an exotic dish.

- *Acquire a favorite perfume; match it with powder and bath salts.*

- *Take long bubble or oil baths, accompanied by a glass of ice cold champagne.*

- *Buy yourself flowers. Often.*

- *Notice the sensuality of your own strength.* Work out, pick a favorite sport to excel in and notice how wonderful you feel mentally and physically as you master it.

- *Get a massage.* Often.

Living Well

avec... La Gentillesse

- *What is the kindest thing anyone has ever done for you?* What was its effect on your life?

- *The infallible "kindness test" in any situation when we are not sure how to behave toward another— How would I like to be treated?*

- *What have you been thinking you should do or would like to do for someone else that would especially please them* but would take an extra effort on your part? When will you do it? Notice how you feel when you do.

- *Each day commit at least one act of kindness.* Anonymous kindnesses count twice!

- *Go on a "Kindness Conquest" once in a while.* Actively look for and commit as many kindnesses as you can in a day or week. Be creative. Have fun.

- *Model kindness for others especially your children.* To teach a child kindness at an early age is to give them a gift that they will continue to give and receive from for the rest of their lives. It will change their world—and ours.

Living Well...
Se Faire Plaisir

- *Putting everyone else's reactions (imagined or real) aside, what are three changes you would like to make in your life?* Pick the first change of the three and break it into "baby steps" to make it easier—mentally and physically.

- *PracAsk Makes Perfect! A huge part of pleasing oneself is asking for what you want*—whether it's a raise at work, or twenty minutes for a bath while a spouse tends the toddler. People aren't mind readers. Plus we often mistakenly assume that our request will be denied, or resented. Don't assume—Ask!

- *Pleasing one's self often means pleasing others less... it's simply part of the territory of taking care of you.* Understand that making yourself a higher priority is not only a new habit for you but for others in your life as well, and that they may (or may not) react in a variety of ways.

- *Know that putting yourself ahead of others, especially if it is a life-long habit, will probably be uncomfortable for you.* Accept that it comes with the territory, just as you'd keep doing those crunches at the gym if you knew you needed them. You can do this—and it will change your life for much the better!

Living Life avec...

Le Calme

- *When anticipating a challenging situation, personal or professional, decide in advance how you will handle it.*

  - Take a step back, to gain perspective on the situation and its importance in the larger scheme of your life.

  - Decide on the ultimate outcome you want to achieve.

  - Decide how you want to be perceived as reacting in the situation.

  - How will you create a sense of partnership with the other(s) ?

- *When a challenging situation is a surprise, do the following –*

  - *Take three deep breaths.* Slowly.

  - *If you can take any kind of break before responding, do so...* even a quick trip to the ladies room or "I'll call you right back," to give yourself time. And do not immediately respond to a (possibly) offending email or text—wait!

- *Speak slowly and clearly, in an even tone.*

- *Do not base or match your reactions on those of others.* Don't meet anger with anger, insult with insult, panic with panic.

- *Assume nothing.* Wait to hear the whole story and assess the situation before reacting .

- *Ask yourself the immediate outcome you desire from this situation.* If possible, decide on the long term outcome as well.

Living Well

avec... la Magie

- *What is the time in your current relationship when you were happiest?*

  - *What attracted you to your beloved?* What was it that made him unique? Which of these things are still true? Let him know what you appreciate/love.

  - *What were the things you most enjoyed doing together?* Make a date to do one or two of these. Make these activities a regular part of your lifestyle again.

  - *What special things did you do for your partner when your relationship was newer?* Enjoy doing them again.

  - *What special things did he do for you that you'd like to request?*

  - *What were you like at that time?* Were you more independent and self sufficient? More spontaneous or physically active? What aspects of yourself do you want to awaken and activate again, for yourself as well as the relationship?

- *Is there any past misunderstanding or mistake that one of you needs to let go of for the health and happiness of your relationship now?* What needs to take place in order for this to happen? For you? For your partner?

Living Well...
avec Pardonner

- *Forgive wrongs for the sake of two people*, yourself as well as the other.

- *Forgive sooner rather than later.* Honor your feelings by allowing time to emotionally process them. Take any actions that are warranted, including talking with the responsible party. Then begin to let go of what happened as rapidly as you realistically can. Bring your mind and your relationship to the present.

- *Discuss what happened with a trusted friend or professional (therapist, coach, priest) in order to process it through.* And when you've processed it, let it go. Repeating it keeps you in "the story" of what happened and devalues the present.

Living Well...
avec la Solitude

- If due to current circumstances you're unable to have an evening or weekend to yourself, *make whatever time you can.* Even an hour alone, a meal alone, is better than no time at all. Schedule and keep this appointment for yourself as seriously as you would any other.

- *Take yourself out for a special dinner alone.* Pick a restaurant you've always wanted to go to, or a favorite. Dress as carefully as you would if you were with a friend or lover. Make a reservation and once there, if you don't like the table you're given, request what you prefer. Take time in ordering your meal and the right wine. Then sit back and savor it, really noticing the nuances of taste and texture. You are required to eat dessert.

- *What are interests of yours that neither your spouse/ lover nor any of your friends share?* What is one activity that you will commit to regularly to appreciate it, alone?

- *Traveling alone is an amazing adventure.* We learn to rely on our own resources and have all sorts of encounters that aren't possible when traveling with two. Something as easy as a road trip to the next town can change your outlook on life as well as encourage you to go farther, for longer next time.

- *Recognize solitude for what it is, a necessity to collect ourselves, know our own minds, reset our priorities.*

Merci Beaucoup to…

French Lessons was fortunate indeed to have had its own godmother, Annabelle Numaguchi.

Annabelle and I met when she became the French "consultant" for the phrasing of FL, but she rapidly became its' muse, present with me for the long distance run that writing a book becomes. In the process she and I were gifted with a close and precious friendship that includes our husbands Manuel and Gen, her children Ella and Miles, and my Beatty (who is *not* a dog.)

My book had its other champions as well. I had two fabulous coaches. Sam Horn was in on the beginning of French Lessons, believed in it and urged me on. Jill Dearman came into my life later and her humor and wisdom helped keep it moving forward. And like all of you, what would I do without my adorable sister/girlfriends? Lisa Albert, Denise Oblak, Judy Sullivan and Heather Carter and others have cheered my writing on.

I must thank she who was my original muse and eternal champion, my precious mother, Pauline Gore McLemore. Mother bestowed on me the three greatest gifts a parent can—love, a spiritual center and the belief that I could accomplish anything if I was determined to do so.

Saving the best for last, I must thank my darling husband, Manuel Davis, who never ceases to support me in whatever crazy dream I pursue or windmill I chose to tilt at. *Je'taime.* You truly *are* the Paris of my heart.

About the author

E. J. Gore, Texan by birth, French by choice, is an author, screenwriter and life coach. Her admiration for women's power to transform themselves and her love for The City of Light, inspired her to write *French Lessons*. She lives in California with her husband Manuel and a Zen Master disguised as a miniature schnauzer, Beatty.

Visit www.frenchlessonstheart.com for more wisdom from Gabrielle and to contact E. J.

43082356R00095

Made in the USA
San Bernardino, CA
14 December 2016